A MIND
UNHINGED

LAWRENCE DRACUT

Copyright Written Work: © Lawrence Dracut 2024

Copyright Cover Page Image: © Ann Brady 2024

Publisher: Pen & Ink Designs Publishing 2024

ISBN: 9781915086150

CONTENTS

FEAR

**_An unpleasant emotion caused by the threat of danger,
pain, or harm._**

"Zoe, are you ready? I hope so or we'll be late, again, and the last time we were, Carlos had already given our time slot to someone else. He also charged us if you remember. We must leave - *now*."

Every Tuesday and Friday for the past six months the sisters had faithfully adhered to a fitness regime. Carried out with the aid of the relentless personal trainer and instructor Carlos, who was South American. Zoe called him 'The Nazi' as he was so demanding, being almost brutal at times. He expected nothing more than 100% obedience from those 'fortunate' enough to be enrolled in his classes. Of course, she never called him that to his face.

Melanie, the younger sibling, not wanting to attend a gym on her own had, over several weeks of nagging, finally persuaded her sister to join her saying, that not only would it improve her health, but it would 'also be fun.'

Which it wasn't, as Zoe would often remind her.

Getting no reply, Melanie made her way into the

spacious kitchen expecting to see her sister dressed and ready to leave, although probably still slumped sleepily over a cup of coffee.

Zoe was not known to be a morning type of person.

Melanie began feeling irritated that not only was Zoe not there, but that she had failed to answer, despite her repeated shouting. There was an eerie silence about the house that Melanie found slightly disturbing.

'Where the hell are you?' she thought as she began looking for Zoe room by room. 'Maybe she's still in bed and has forgotten to set the alarm? Or maybe Anthony, her husband, didn't wake her before he left for work?'

Not to be found anywhere on the lower floor Melanie made her way upstairs, knocking grumpily on the master bedroom door, while simultaneously calling her sister's name.

Receiving no answer, she cautiously opened the door and glanced around the room. At first, she thought it was empty, however, the bed was unmade which was unlike her fastidious sister. But her puzzlement was short-lived as she was soon to see why.

There in the far corner of the room, curled up into a tight ball, her knees drawn up against her chest, was Zoe. Melanie nearly went into a state of shock, not only at finding her sister in this condition but at seeing her sister's beautiful long red hair was now as white as snow.

Kneeling next to her she cradled her sibling gently, not knowing what to say. Melanie only knew that she needed to comfort her. Trying to hold Zoe tight proved not an easy task due to the violent trembling of her body.

At first, there was no recognition as to who it was that was holding her. Zoe feebly tried to fight Melanie off; a look of primordial fear emanating from her eyes. Then eventually she recognised who was embracing her. Beginning to sob and with her body still shaking she managed, in a quivering voice, to utter a few words.

"They've taken him. They have taken, Anthony." She continued to cry.

While cuddling her sister with one arm, Melanie used her free hand to retrieve her mobile phone from the back pocket of her jeans, deftly dialling emergency services. Giving the address of her location she calmly requested an ambulance, then as a second thought, said, "We also need the police, as I think there has been a kidnapping."

It was only moments ago that Melanie had arrived

expecting to be here with just enough time to collect Zoe, so she had left the front door open. This was fortunate as she would not have to leave her sister's side for even a moment to allow the paramedics' entry.

Appearing a lot sooner than anticipated, Melanie was relieved to hear them announce their arrival. She responded in a now shaky voice loudly, "We are upstairs, please hurry."

Almost at the same time as the medics entered, they were followed by a uniformed officer and a weather-beaten-looking plainclothes detective, who identified himself as Inspector Hoshiko.

"Are you the lady who called?" he asked. Melanie nodded.

With a cursory look around the room, and seeing the paramedics had the situation under control, Hoshiko took charge of Melanie. "I think we should go downstairs, let them do their job, while you tell me what is going on."

His voice sounded like that of someone who was used to taking command of any situation. His reassuring tone meant Melanie was slowly coming to terms with the events of the past half an hour, even though she still had no understanding of what had happened upstairs.

Realising she was still trembling Melanie was glad of the Inspector's arm to lean on as they made their way down the staircase and into the living room. Gently but firmly, he manoeuvred her across to one of the overstuffed chesterfield chairs.

"Sit down and try and relax?" he instructed. "Once you are ready, you can tell me who you are, why you are here, and what you think has happened."

Melanie used the back of her hand to try and stem the flow of tears that were now cascading down her cheeks. She was grateful for the handkerchief offered to her by Hoshiko. Then, taking a breath she began explaining who she was and why she was here at this time in the morning.

Then she told him how she had found her sister. It took barely five minutes.

"So, that's all she has said since you arrived?" asked the detective. "Just, the words 'they have taken him.' I assume he is her husband."

Feeling calmer but still unable to stop the trickle of tears Melanie merely nodded in reply.

Inspector Hoshiko sat motionless, studying the young woman sitting opposite him. He waited patiently while his sole witness to whatever had happened in this house calmed down and composed herself.

He had quickly assessed the situation. Other than a very distressed woman who had uttered a few words, and her compassionate sister, there did not seem a lot to investigate.

Once slightly more relaxed Melanie spoke.

"There is one more extremely important point I haven't mentioned Inspector. Yesterday, my sister, the woman you briefly saw upstairs. When I last saw her, she had dazzling red hair; not the white colour that you saw!" She stopped to take a shuddering breath. "Something so terrifying must have happened overnight that the pure fear of it caused that change in her. Who, or what, in God's name could have possibly occurred for that to happen to her?"

Oddly enough Hoshiko did not seem to question what he had just been told. Instead, he looked intently at Melanie as now it was his turn to compose himself before he prepared to speak. Eventually he began to tell something that would surprise and probably leave her confused.

"You may be surprised to know that I have no doubt that everything you have told me is true. This is not the only time I have had experience of this phenomenon. Err... I remember something very similar when I was a child."

Here he paused, in order to choose his words carefully.

"So, you must first realise that I am not unsympathetic to what you are going through. I can tell you about that incident; if you would like me to?"

"Please do," replied Melanie.

"I recall I was about nine or ten years old at the time. Living next door to my home was a family that included three teenage girls. I wouldn't like to say that they were exceptionally unruly but, even at my tender age, I did think them a bit wild, to put it mildly. They were known to smoke the odd joint, or take an occasional hit of LSD, and so forth." He paused, allowing these actions to settle in Melanie's mind.

"There was no fatherly presence in the house, so I suppose it must have been difficult for a single mother to work and control her little family. The particular night to which I am referring, sometime after midnight, and after their mother had gone to bed, they decided to dabble in one of the dark arts. By this, I mean the use of a Ouija board they had somehow got their hands on."

"Oh no," Melanie interrupted. "I have also known a few people who have tried that, and it scared them to death. Sorry, please continue."

"Of course, I have no idea how long they had been attempting to contact the spirit world, but at about 2 am I was woken abruptly from a deep sleep by lots of loud hysterical screaming. It was coming from their house and sounded almost maniacal in tone." He shuddered as recalled the sound of that night.

"I remember running into my parent's bedroom to see my father already putting his trousers and shirt on. Quickly telling me to go back to my room he left, running towards next-door. I don't know who called them, but it wasn't long before their house was surrounded by all kinds of cars and vehicles with flashing lights. Obviously, it was the police and ambulance services." The Inspector paused as remembered that night of fear.

"My father came back home about an hour later, but he would never talk about what had happened to our neighbours. Later, I did overhear some of what he told my mother.

Arriving at the house he pounded his fist frantically on the front door, which was soon opened by the girl's mother. Wordlessly she beckoned him to go upstairs. He had, he said, pushed open the bedroom door and was shocked to see all three girls sitting on the floor, huddled together, screaming and crying; and yes, you may have guessed it, all three had pure white hair. I used to see them often on my way to school, and I remember that two of them had black hair, and the third girls was brown."

"After that night I never saw them again. Within a couple of weeks, they had moved out of our neighbourhood. That night, and anything to do with it, was a strictly forbidden subject in our house; never to be spoken of. As a child, I was left to imagine what unspeakable horrors they must have endured."

Once again, he paused, and another slight shudder seemed to run down his spine. Gathering his thoughts he continued. "Periodically, as I got older, I would look at what little research there was available on this subject. This is what I have learnt. Indescribable fear causes the sympathetic nervous system, which is responsible for our bodies' involuntary responses, to become hyperactive."

Melanie looked at Hoshiko quizzically as he continued to explain. "When this happens it, in turn, drives rapid depletion of the stem cells that are responsible for hair colour. The result is an instantaneous pigmentation loss in the hair."

"So, if I understand you correctly," Melanie surmised, "then whatever it was that caused this to happen to your neighbours must have been equally as terrifying for my sister."

"Yes, I believe so," answered Hoshiko. "We can only hope that one day she will overcome whatever it was that scared her so badly." But despite his positive response, as he said it, there was a tone of pity in his voice perhaps him knowing that she most likely never would."

He smiled warmly to try and take the sting from his response. Then he became businesslike and put on his Inspector hat once again.

"Now, back to the current situation. There does not appear to be any obvious crime scene here. No break-in, no blood, nothing that warrants an immediate police presence. All we have at this moment in time is a woman who is now under sedation, and possibly a husband that has disappeared in the middle of the night. Sorry."

Standing he smiled warmly again at Melanie, as if to allay any further fears she might have. He did not do a good job.

"When I get back to the station I will list your brother-in-law as a missing person. Hopefully tomorrow, I will be able to interview your sister at the hospital if, of course, she can speak."

Upstairs the wailing had finally subsided as the sedative took effect. This meant the paramedics were now in the process of securing her to a stretcher ready for her journey to the hospital.

"I assume that you will be going directly to the hospital?" inquired the Inspector.

Melanie nodded.

"When she wakes up, please call me immediately and I will meet you there. Here is my mobile number," and he handed her his card. Hoshiko then called his uniformed assistant and they left.

Melanie, making sure the house was secure and all the doors were locked left soon afterwards.

* * * * *

At the hospital, Melanie had been sitting next to her sister's bed for several anxious hours. Occasionally she clutched Zoe's hand when she sensed an involuntary rigidity in her body, for even in her sedated condition, she was still recalling whatever had frightened her.

Eventually, she stirred. Her eyes opening wide, she lay there for the rest of the day in a state that can only be described as catatonic.

It was early evening when Melanie, weary through lack of sleep finally heard her sister's voice. She spoke clearly but in a timbre that still betrayed a modicum of fear, as if she was still unsure of her safety even in this seemingly secure hospital.

As she spoke, what she related to Melanie sounded like the ramblings of someone who was in dire need of Psychiatric help. However, knowing how emotionally stable Zoe had always been, Melanie just listened patiently to every single disturbing word.

Between brief bouts of weeping the events of the previous night were slowly recalled.

"It was about one in the morning," she began. "We had

just gone to bed, having stayed up later than usual to watch a sci-fi movie on Netflix. Anthony had just turned off the bedside table lamp when, in the corner by the closet door, a strange pale silvery light appeared. It stretched from the ceiling to the floor, and at first, it seemed like a mist wavering like a ripple would across a calm pond."

She paused momentarily, as if she was too scared to speak of what had happened, but then doggedly she carried on.

"Slowly two beings emerged from this undulating curtain, they looked human-like but were tall and extremely thin. Their skin was pale… almost colourless. At first, I thought that I was imagining everything. I mean, we had just been watching a futuristic film, but as I turned towards Anthony the look on his face told me that it was all real."

"We couldn't move or speak. I don't know if this was out of fear or whether they had done something to us. It was like… being paralysed. Neither of the creatures spoke, and yet I could understand what they were saying to me. It must have been some powerful kind of telepathy for not only was I able to understand what they wanted me to know, but they also understood my thoughts; even as they were forming in my mind."

Zoe swallowed as she recalled the experience, then she continued. "My mind was racing as I wanted to ask, 'Are you, aliens, from another planet? 'What do you want? Are you going to harm us?'"

Again, she stopped speaking, shuddering as she gasped to breathe more easily, but then she continued.

"Their faces were expressionless as my thoughts were answered immediately. 'We are not aliens', they transmitted to me. 'And we do not come from another planet as some other life forms do'. 'No. We belong here the same as you.' I was shocked but before I could speak, they responded again, answering my unspoken question, - 'How can that be possible?'"

At this point, Zoe stopped speaking and looked at her sister, as if expecting her to answer the question.

Receiving no response, she went on shakily, "The one that looked slightly taller of the two was the one that I think was communicating with me, and although it was given to me telepathically, I was aware of its displeasure. He, she, or whatever it was, looked at us as if we were nothing more than an inferior underdeveloped lower form of life."

The look of sheer horror on her sister's face caused Melanie to feel unsettled.

Finally, her sister continued. "Then in my mind, it said, 'Do you really believe, because you can only see what is around you, that you are the only species that exists? This parallel universe that we share is one of many thousands that are inhabited by numerous other species, some like us, although they exist in different dimensions.'"

"I knew I was trembling with fear but still, my mind was teeming with questions. They must have sensed this, yet before I could ask anything more, I began to experience a mass of information being sent to me. I suppose similar to what you get when downloading a file onto a computer. I am never going to be able to forget any of it, even if I wanted to. It is as if it is forever imprinted on my memory."

The thoughts of all she knew and could not forget brought tears to Zoe's eyes. Eventually she calmed herself and carried on explaining.

"I know that this will sound like me giving you a short lesson in physics, but this is what I was told. 'The world as we know it is made up of three dimensions, Space-length, width and depth, and one dimension of time. That is all we are aware of. Yet, in reality, this universe is just like every other universe. They are all made up of infinitesimal vibrating strings, countless times smaller than atoms. As these strings constantly vibrate, they twist and fold, producing many universes of varying sizes that frequently warp into each other. And it is when this happens that other species from alternate dimensions can cross over into our reality."

And here she paused to take a deep breath.

"However," Zoe added, "I was also told that they usually choose the night-time to cross over as it is quieter, and they are then less likely to be seen, unless they want to be. Plus, as well as all these other beings, it is also the time when the good, or evil spirit forms of our deceased can appear to us as well."

At this point Melanie was unsure whether what she was hearing was sense or the mad ravings of a mind that had been warped by fear. All she could do was sit and listen, allowing her sister to talk the horror out of her system. Hopefully for some solution and peace.

Looking straight into her sister's eyes, Zoe calmly told

Melanie, "As I was being inundated with all this knowledge, I had temporarily overcome my initial fear, but then the realism of what I had learnt started to fill me with dread. That is, that at any time, any one of us could be subject to an unwanted nocturnal visit, from the spirits or beings that may or may not be friendly."

The look on her sister's face caused Melanie to shudder but she couldn't speak as Zoe continued talking.

"But there was still more I was to learn as the being continued. 'There are those who have wanted to make the transition from their dimension into this one permanent. And so, they have been living amongst you as humans for many centuries of your years. Their reason for doing this I will not disclose, only that they live and work harmoniously alongside humans in your society.' At this point it stopped transmitting as its companion must have indicated something. Finally, he continued, telling me, 'We must leave now, as our time in this dimension is limited, so our visits are brief; but we will return as we always have in the past. Your breeding mate will be returned in a few days, but for now, he is needed by our females.' Hearing those words in my head I immediately looked to my left," Zoe cried, "but Anthony had vanished, and as I looked back, at the same time so had the two beings."

She paused once more, then displayed a look of foreboding before carrying on. "I was told that of the countless other species that inhabit these other dimensions, not all of them are friendly. I was given an image that made me think that for some of them, the reasons for their visits were not for our benefit but were, in fact, hostile, menacing, and possibly destructive."

Shivering again, Zoe carried on speaking. "Mel, now that I have been given all this incredible knowledge, there is one thing that scares me the most and always will. I know that any time, any of one or more of those 'things' can appear whenever they want. Especially while we are asleep."

Finally, sounding exhausted, Zoe stopped speaking and tears slowly began to course down her face as she thought about what had happened to her and her husband.

Melanie wanted to take her sister in her arms yet didn't know how or if she could offer her in the form of real comfort.

Finally, Zoe checked herself and spoke again. "I know that if I am ever to see Anthony again, I must go back to the house. But how will I ever be able to sleep knowing that I will be constantly looking towards the corner of that room, waiting for that misty curtain to appear? And if, or when it does return, will it be my husband that comes out of it, or will it be some kind of demonic creature that only wants to harm me?"

Unnoticed by either of the sisters, Inspector Hoshiko had earlier slipped into the room. He had been sitting quietly in the corner listening, occasionally frowning. Hearing all that had been said and believing that Zoe had now finished, he poked his head around the partially closed curtain, which was around Zoe's bed.

"Good evening, ladies."

Then, addressing Zoe, he said, "I am pleased to see that you are starting to recover from the heavy sedative you received last night. I did not expect your sister to think about calling me until she was at first content with your condition and had been able to speak to you. I understand that you are her priority, so I decided to save her a phone call."

Pausing, he thought carefully before deciding how to broach the next subject.

Finally, he said, "I must admit that I have been listening

to everything you have told your sister and I have no doubt that you have accurately described what you went through last night. I wish to reassure you that I am extremely understanding of your situation. However, after considering what few available facts there are, my conclusion is that there is no evidence that a crime has been committed which, unfortunately means I am unable to investigate any further."

Hoshiko paused, waiting for the inevitable outcry of 'surely there was something he could do.' However, there was only silence from the two women, so he continued speaking.

"The only verifiable details that I can put in my report is that an ambulance was requested to attend your house and that you were sedated, before being brought to this hospital. Plus, of course, that your husband is also missing, and will be registered as such. Based on what you were told I understood he will probably be returned to you sooner or later."

Again, he waited for a response.

Once more with nothing from either lady, he continued. "With all of this in mind, I would like to offer you a sincere piece of advice. Besides the two of you, and of course myself, no one knows anything about what happened to you, and I can see no advantage to you in revealing it to anyone else at all. Based on my experience, the parasites in the media, if they were to find out, would love it. However, you would end up being hounded by the press and television, before eventually being labelled as a crackpot. Unfortunately, that is what people do when something like this is beyond their comprehension. Personally, I think it would be best if you were to both keep it to yourselves. But that is your choice to make not mine."

Having said his piece, the Inspector wished them well and made his way towards the door. Stopping, he looked back at Zoe, saying," So that you do not feel alone in your new enlightenment of this world, let me assure you that I too know that what are called 'aliens' do live here on this planet, and within this reality. I also know that they have been here for many years, working side by side with everyone else, just as your visitors explained to you."

Opening the door, he was about to leave when he was stopped by Melanie, saying, "Thank you Inspector for being so considerate and understanding. There is one last thing I would like to ask you, if it is not too personal a question. I have been meaning to ask about your name. It sounds

Japanese, and yet, obviously, you are not?"

Smiling, the Inspector took a moment to reply. "You are correct, and I do not mind answering you. Hoshiko is, in fact, an ancient Japanese name that has two similar meanings. One is a 'star', and the other is... 'a spirit from the universe'!"

"Oh, and by the way, one more thing," he added as he started closing the door. "The 'aliens' that have been living here for thousands of years! Most of them are nice and friendly, have families, and responsible jobs. Some of them even enjoy successful careers in law enforcement."

And he winked as he left.

OH, FOR GOD'S SAKE

When you need to talk to other beings!

Yesterday morning I talked to God! I don't mean in the usual way that most people do. I wasn't kneeling by my bed praying, I just… talked to him.

Well, I think I did.

I was sitting at my desk as normal, coffee in front of me just wondering if I was going to start writing another novel, or as the sun was beckoning me to go outside, maybe I should walk the dog. Any excuse to procrastinate? If there was a prize for that I would most definitely win first place.

Suddenly I heard this commanding but calm and gentle voice from somewhere in the room, but before I could turn around to see where it was coming from, I was told to sit still and not speak for a moment. Strangely, I obeyed.

"I do not want you to be afraid," the voice said, "but I am the one you all call, God."

For some unknown reason, I remained calm and listened.

"Every thousand years or so the wife reminds me that I must visit this planet and check up on how you are all progressing. You know what's it's like to have a wife; better to do what they say and get it over with. So, reluctantly here I am again."

By this time, I had found my voice, daring to speak. "Why me, why did you pick me?" I stammered.

"Frankly, I didn't select you specifically, but she reminded me that on my last two visits, I met with women. This time, she said, that I should select someone who was about average, not very intelligent, and insignificant, so choose a man. You fit the requirements perfectly. I do not intend to be here for longer than necessary so let's get on with it. Ask what you want, and I will try to answer in a way that your primal brain can understand."

Trying hard not to feel insulted I struggled to get my first question out, managing to utter, "If you only visit us once every thousand years, approximately, why this specific time?"

"Mmm… this will require a long answer so sit tight and

wait for me to finish. I have been informed that you, and by you, I mean every human being on this planet, have made a total mess of things. I needed to see how badly and if the reports were accurate. Sadly, I can see that they are correct."

"I do remember when I first created this planet and what a beautiful place it was. I put all types of exotic and beautiful creatures on every continent, and I caused wonderful trees and edible plants to grow equally. Also, there were bushes with delicious fruit on them. They were there for the animals to eat but were so wonderful one could simply admire them; such was their beauty. For eons, I was pleased and satisfied with my efforts."

"However, after a few millennia had passed I must admit I was gullible enough to take advice from one of my most trusted helpers, those you call angels. His name was Yaldabaoth; you know him as Lucifer. He advised that as I didn't visit here very often, that maybe all I had created should be enjoyed by some other type of life form. It seemed such a pity to waste it all on just the animals."

Lucifer said he could create others, suggesting he introduce carnivorous animals. They would keep the planet free of disease by eating the sickly, injured creatures and would ensure that the population was kept at a manageable level. I am afraid I agreed, instructing him to go ahead."

Sighing, God said, "Considering that I am omnipotent I fell for all he said, even agreeing to his second suggestion. And so, I commanded him to create mankind."

"Now that was probably the biggest mistake I have ever made. Especially, as within just a few generations, you started fighting and quarrelling with each other. You took possessions that did not belong to you and even started killing animals for food. This has really annoyed me since there was so much choice in the abundant vegetation. You have defiled paradise."

"Do you know that I began to dislike you? I even thought about completely wiping you all off the planet and starting again. I will admit I did try out that plan on a small scale with a bit of a flood, but it made a mess of the landscape, so I changed my mind."

"Mmm…of course, it became clear after a while what my little angel of light wanted all along. He had become bored with being my trusted helper and wanted somewhere to call his own. Somewhere he could rule over and have fun with.

So, when I discovered this, I threw him and his minions out of our heavenly abode, telling him he could never return as he had betrayed me."

"Problem is, I have so many other worlds to care for that I could no longer spend any more time here. I left him and this planet, vowing to return every thousand years to survey what had become of Lucifer and what was now his sole domain…"

"What do I call you?" I interrupted. "Every religion calls you by a different name; Yaweh, Jehovah, Elohim, Adonai, Allah, Shiva, Atten, and dozens more. Why did you start so many different religions?"

"This will require a somewhat longer answer, and it goes back to Lucifer again. It was not long before he had once more become bored. He had always been mean-spirited but by now he was becoming extremely bloodthirsty. It was getting more difficult to start wars, which seemed to be his favourite pastime. He had to think of new ways to entertain himself."

"Now, it seemed he had for several years persuaded one very large group of people to build this massive tower in a futile attempt to reach heaven. It wasn't possible of course; it was just his way of annoying me. Once this tower, you people called it Babel, was almost complete he, not me as many of you think, caused everyone who had worked on it to start speaking in dozens of different languages. It was absolute chaos. This seemed to appease his sense of humour. Eventually, though he needed something else to keep himself occupied. It was then he formulated the most diabolical and destructive idea his malevolent mind could spawn. He created religion."

Here God seemed to appear annoyed at both Lucifer and his own stupidity! However, he continued speaking to me.

"Lucifer had already disrupted the civilizations with his multi-language concept, so it was relatively easy to give mankind new beliefs and ideas, forcing these groups even further apart. To one tribe he would give certain commands and instructions, then totally different ones to another tribe, and so on and so on. Of course, every tribe was then convinced that their beliefs and way of life were the right ones."

"Then he further commanded that they write it all down in various forms so it would carry on religiously forever."

God suddenly laughed. "My little joke there! However,

to continue. Several leaders were appointed to ensure that every command he gave them was adhered to as given them. These leaders called themselves prophets, which gave them a sense of self-importance. But here comes the best bit, and I have to admire his ingenuity for this, he said that all of this came from me."

I was gob smacked. Was God really admitting that he wasn't to blame for this disruption?

"Oh!" he went on, "I almost forgot to tell you. There were never any physical manifestations at all, ever, to anyone, anywhere. It was all accomplished through dreams or visions. Of course, mankind being a simple primitive life form listened to what they believed came from me, God! Who could say it didn't? To deny that would be a punishable sin. I must say that was a brilliant move on his part." And here God chuckled.

"And so, for the next few thousand years, wars were fought, lands invaded, millions of people killed, and all done in my name. Strangely, I don't have a name. I am quite content to be known as 'I AM', or the omnipotent one.!

"Of course, that meant he could tell them anything he wanted, always giving the instructions through a man, my prophets! Lucifer was probably the first misogynist. Or, maybe he just took advantage of the fact that most men are extremely gullible. And, as everyone was now speaking a different language it was easy to tell one group this is God's name, that he has caused to be written in such a way, and this is how you should worship if you want to please him."

"Later, he would go to a different tribe, give them a different name for me, and a different book of instruction. All for the purpose of furthering enmity between mankind. He must have enjoyed himself doing this."

I was beginning to despair. No wonder we were in a mess. If God couldn't sort us out, then how could we sort ourselves?

God went on speaking. "Worst of all he even persuaded several of these groups to kill anyone that did not follow the same commands that had been written for them. They became so eager to please, that some even prayed to me, asking for help in their monstrous and mindless endeavours to slaughter any man, woman, or child that did not share their incredulous beliefs."

It was here that I had become nervous for God had raised his voice. Not a lot, but enough for me to sense that he was angry. I will admit to a slight trembling of my entire body as he continued speaking.

"Why would I be pleased in the destruction of what I had caused to be created? I create, I do not destroy!" he bellowed.

He calmed himself a little and carried on.

"But, to get back to you, young man, it is time for me to leave. I think you have just enough intelligence to realise that currently there is a lot of work to be done in this world that you live in. I no longer have the patience, or desire to do anything about it or even talk about it."

"However, I will shortly remove Lucifer and his followers from this place and find a nice barren but habitable planet for them to live on. So, no more influence or interference from anyone. You will all be on your own. Which means, that what happens next is entirely up to you and your fellow man, and, of course, fellow woman."

I will, of course, return in another millennium. It will be interesting to see if you have made any progress at all, or if there is even anything left of this once beautiful planet. I do hope there is as I don't want to start over from scratch. Oh, remember, you all have eternal souls, so make of that what you will!"

And abruptly I was once again on my own.

My coffee had gone cold, and the sun was beginning to set. I have no idea how long I had been sitting there. I do know that I felt troubled as I tried to make sense of the past lost hours. Had God really spoken to me, or was I suddenly having visions and dreams like the prophets of old? Or maybe I was having an episode of schizophrenia? It was all too much for my fragile mind to bear.

So, I decided to take the dog for a walk.

DREAMING

Are dreams always what they should be?

Not everyone dreams. Yet, of those who do, only fragments remain of what they imagined during their slumbers. However, there are also those few whose dreams are quite vivid, often being extremely realistic, and sometimes even frightening. Dreams that can remain with them during their waking hours.

For the past twenty-plus years of her adult life, Bethany had often experienced perplexing and weird dreams. However, there were two, that in slightly diverse forms, seemed to occur more often than most. Ones that she had strangely become accustomed to having.

These dreams were often accompanied by a faceless, nameless passenger who, somehow, felt familiar, meaning she would soon be lost in another world. But, true to her lifestyle, these dreams would not be similar to those of less fortunate people.

Oh no.

Instead, it was as if Bethany was lost in a luxury car of some description, more often than not a Mercedes or a Jaguar. And always along with her anonymous companion, who continually offered suggestions for shortcuts. Which meant that the pair inevitably wandered further and further away from their original destination.

Sometimes they were in a wooded mountain region which would then, bizarrely, become a dusty high desert from where they could see their destination in the valley down below. However, the twists and turns made during their descent predictably always took them miles away from home.

The second dream was of a similar nature, but this one was more localised.

Here, Bethany would find herself in the car, once more with the same individual, but it was he who was now the driver. Now they were simply driving around the town in an endless search for her car.

Numerous car parks were usually visited, with some being on small muddy hillsides. Whilst others were big-tarmacked affairs; often having the occasional clueless parking attendant in attendance. Regardless, the results were always the same. Bethany never managed to return home. Nor did she ever find her car.

Instead, she would wake up with a feeling of frustration and disappointment, yet always feeling relieved that it was only just a dream.

Bethany had long since learnt to accept that she was the owner of an extremely active mind, who would frequently hold intelligent conversations with the participants of her dreams. Nothing unusual about that, I suppose. However, upon waking, this would usually leave her feeling fatigued and bemused.

Several years ago and wanting to seek an explanation for these nighttime disturbances, Bethany had consulted a therapist who specialised in the interpretation of recurring dreams.

His analysis and subsequent explanation were that there had been something missing in her life for a long time, and it was this that was encouraging her constant need to search. Unfortunately, exactly what she was seeking for he did not have an answer. And so, her dreams had continued.

Then, last night something strange had happened. The dream had been different.

In it, she had woken unexpectedly, being bewildered to discover a small group of familiar people standing at the side of her bed. No one moved. They were all simply stood, silently watching her.

Knowing it was yet another dream, Bethany was not afraid at being confronted by the apparitions her tired mind had conjured up, even though there was one peculiarity they all shared.

You see, for some strange reason, they all appeared to have her face. Although, they were all slightly different as they appeared to emanate from several stages of her life. From her early childhood up to her being a middle-aged adult.

In her dreamlike state, Bethany serenely addressed the gathered host.

"Who are you and why are you here? You are disturbing my sleep."

Her question was answered by the more prominent of them, a tall, stern, and imposing figure. In a voice that was slightly unworldly, and yet quite similar to her own, it answered.

"We are you, or rather we are your consciousness."

"What! But why so many?" she asked. "I always imagined that everyone only had one, or maybe two - depending on whether you had both a good and a bad side to your personality."

"That is what most people perceive. However, in reality,

it involves every major part of your personality. Your past deeds, and your major events - good or bad They are all broken up into all these separate life forms you see before you," answered the spiritual-sounding voice. "Each one of them must be revisited."

One of the visions at the back of the crowd spoke next.

"You recently had an affair that resulted in a marriage breaking up, how do you feel about that now?"

Surprised that this part of her life should be so abruptly examined Bethany thought, before hastily answering.

"His wife was horrible to him. She publicly belittled him, refusing to show him love, ever, and love was something he needed, and it was what I could give him," she replied defiantly.

However, the interrogator went on.

"But, Bethany, what about all the other affairs you have had with married men, how can you justify those? And, how can you explain the five times you were engaged to be married? Was it so you could get expensive rings that you could then sell for large amounts of money? Be honest, it was, wasn't it?"

"W... well, umm...," she stammered as her mind

desperately scrambled for a believable reason to defend her actions.

Having failed to find one, and trying to change the subject, she fought back with, "Why don't you ask me about all the good things I have done in my life? I have done so much for animal charities, volunteered to Help the Aged, and done all kinds of good and generous works."

"Yes, that is true," exclaimed another voice from the rear of the crowd, as if supporting her. "I do recall the many times she has rescued defenceless and injured animals from their cruel owners. Although… I am also aware that her selfish side has far exceeded her caring side."

For what seemed to Bethany to be an eternity, the different parts of her conscience appeared to offer up both good and bad significant incidents of her past life.

Some of these pleased her but, more often than not, they made her end up having to robustly defend her actions about what was said.

By now, Bethany, was starting to feel irritated by this bizarre dream, which was quickly becoming more of a nightmare, so she declared to the crowd, "Stop! I have had enough. I need to resume my normal sleep so, if you will all kindly leave me alone now, please."

All at once the nocturnal visitors began laughing in unison, even the younger ones, until one of them spoke again.

"You still don't get it, do you, Bethany? You are never going to go back to sleep, ever again."

"And why is that?" she questioned, with an edge of mockery to her voice.

"Because, my dear girl... you are dead! D-E-A-D - dead," came the equally sarcastic reply.

At this moment, Bethany's confrontational side came to the fore as she almost shouted, "Don't be so stupid, I can't be, I'm only forty-two years old. Of course, I am not dead, how can I be?"

Yet another voice addressed her, saying, "Maybe it has something to do with your lifestyle. You've been smoking twenty cigarettes a day, eaten mostly takeaway meals, and have never properly exercised a day in your life."

"Oh, and let's not forget that she drank like the proverbial fish," said another. "Besides, if you don't believe us just turn around and look at your bed."

Feeling insulted by the remark about her alcohol abuse, Bethany nevertheless did as instructed and slowly turned around.

Looking at the bed she gasped. There, lying peacefully on the bed was her body, looking as if she was still asleep. Also, after a closer look she noticed there was no visible evidence of the heart attack that had supposedly taken her in the middle of the night.

"I know this is only another one of my bemusing dreams. So, IF I am truly dead, what will happen next? Have I been judged? Will I be whisked off to some heavenly plane, maybe shot up a tunnel of light to meet Jesus?" she asked sneeringly.

The answer swiftly came back.

"Oh, no. No tunnel of light, no meeting Jesus, or anyone at all. No heaven or hell even. For you, there is nothing, just us. From now on, every single moment you will relive this night. Our conversations, our accusations, and your defensive replies. This is it for you... forever."

Suddenly Bethany woke up.

"Oh, thank God that's over," she mumbled to herself. "I hope I never have another bloody dream like that one," and she laughed.

"Getting lost and driving around for hours in a car doesn't seem too bad a dream after a nightmare like that. Mmm... I think that later today I will phone the therapist again and make an appointment. It will be worth the £50 to find out what the hell this latest dream is all about."

And as she sat on the edge of her bed, momentarily rubbing the sleep from her eyes, she giggled a little.

Eventually, her bleary vision was drawn to the other side of the bedroom, which suddenly appeared to be growing menacingly dark and gloomy.

At first, she was bewildered by the emergence of the same group of spectral beings that her collective conscience had disturbed her sleep with last night. Then, simultaneously she became aware of the mild pain in her chest that was constricting her breathing.

Gradually the inevitable horrifying truth dawned on her.

" No, No, No, please, it can't be……!

ONE LAST TRIP FOR JACOB

Going places we expect to come back from!

CHAPTER ONE

Six foot one, a hundred and sixty pounds, short blond hair, and a shallow complexion. Also, a junkie, a high school dropout, and a deadbeat. All this added up to the being that was Jacob Thomson, one of life's born losers. He was also destined to never amount to anything more than this, even if he were to live beyond his nineteenth birthday, which he wouldn't.

For several weeks he had been living in his car. It had was once been a classic Chevy Impala in a stunning shade of metallic green. Now, it was predominantly shades of rust due to Jacob's neglect.

Mechanically it still possessed most of its proud heritage. Fitted with one of Detroit's finest 460 cubic inch V8 engines, it could still blow the doors off almost any Japanese imports now flooding the streets of Salt Lake City.

Not out of choice had the Chevy become his new abode, but such a decision had been based on the notion that he would no longer choose to be his father's main source of income. The money that he did reluctantly give him was used for the sole purpose of buying the old man's daily requirements of cheap liquor, thus making him officially classed as an alcoholic.

Constant verbal abuse and the occasional beer can, empty of course, thrown at his head or in his general direction, finally confirmed Jacob's decision to move out of the only home he had ever known. His dad's dilapidated double-wide caravan at Meadow Creek trailer park.

He would leave asap.

Stealing enough to feed his own growing habit was dodgy enough, but having to provide for his father's ever-increasing drinking needs was only adding to the risks he had to take. Especially as the 'top of the line' car stereos were only fetching 20 to 25 dollars apiece at the pawn shops he favoured dealing with. This meant he had to average about twenty-five break-ins a week just to supply himself with cheap beer and whatever the day's drug of choice was. Plus, of course, the daily minimum of fast food to keep his scrawny body alive.

Finally, when Jacob could not see one good reason why he should continue living with his dead-beat dad, it wasn't a difficult decision for him to up sticks and move.

Jacob had stood staring down at Jacob Senior who was passed out, recuperating on the only half-decent piece of furniture he still owned. Sadly it looked only a little less worn and lifeless than its present occupier. After packing his few meagre possessions into a canvas backpack he prepared to say a silent farewell, forever.

Before he left, Jacob took one final glance at the tarnished silver picture frame that contained the only known photograph of his mother, Kitty. She too had suddenly, although not unexpectedly, left this miserable place. Leaving only a brief note, she had explained that she could no longer be expected to be the sole provider from her salary as a waitress. She had planned on starting a new and wonderful life for herself as far away from Salt Lake City. Somewhere sunny and warm.

'I want to meet new people, have new experiences, and make new friends,' she had concluded the note.

According to the occasional reports Jacob had heard about her, she had indeed made new friends. But only for about 15 to 30 minutes at a time, and mainly along the truck stops on the interstate highways. Although aged about forty, and now working the world's oldest profession, her expected lifespan was probably not going to remain a long one. However, she would still outlive her son by about twenty years.

Finally, quietly and gingerly he picked up his mother's picture, smiled, and then casually dropped it in the trash can just outside the trailer door.

"Screw you too, ya bitch," he muttered and left.

CHAPTER TWO

Two days before leaving Meadow Creek, which incidentally was not a picturesque meadow or anywhere near flowing water of any kind, Jacob had pulled off one of his favorite and most profitable rip- offs.

He had desperately needed a sleeping bag, especially if he was to sleep comfortably in the back of the Chevy, but as usual, he had neither the cash nor the desire to pay for one anyway.

It is common knowledge to most shoppers, that the large department stores always have their Major and Small Appliance departments situated at the rear of the building. They want to encourage their customers to pay for their goods from these sections at 'conveniently 'located check-out counters within the departments. This supposedly relieves some of the pressure on the main checkout areas located at the store's exits, especially during busy peak periods.

Large items, such as televisions and microwaves were identified as 'paid for' by the department check-out staff by placing several brightly coloured stickers on the box, that identified the item as 'paid.'

That way Security staff could then see at a glance that the item had indeed already been paid for, thus allowing the customer to walk past the main check-out area and straight out the door.

Of course, the so-called security experts had not considered people like Jacob. Ones, who would habitually scan people's trash whenever he was walking or driving through the more affluent neighbourhoods.

On these occasions, when he spotted a discarded cardboard box that had recently contained an item of value, he knew there was every possibility that the highly sought-after sticker was still on it. He would collect as many of these labels as he could find, if not for immediate use, then for the future when he needed to supplement his income.

The stickers came in several colours and sizes, with the stores changing them on a regular basis in their pointless attempts to avoid security breaches. This week the colour was orange, oval, and about the same diameter as a can of Dr Pepper.

The sticker that had been used for this latest acquisition, he recalled with misguided pride, he had carefully removed from a box that had contained a 32- inch Panasonic television.

He also remembered with amusement a lengthy discussion that had taken place between himself and a sales clerk in the sporting goods section as he had 'persuaded Jacob to go for the more expensive Icelandic Mummy sleeping bag. Although bulky and more expensive he was assured that it was well worth the extra money. After thanking the salesman for his advice and help, Jacob said that he would pay for the item with the rest of the shopping he still had to do, at the main exit.

Casually walking through two adjacent departments, he turned left by the cosmetics counter and then straight down the main aisle. Slowing his pace just a little gave him enough time to reach inside his Parka coat to remove two of this week's current labels. Placing them in a conspicuous part of his 'purchase' Jacob smiled back at the store greeter, who with as much a fake sincerity as she could muster, thanked him for shopping with us, and adding "Have a nice day."

CHAPTER THREE

"Hey, dumb ass." Even before he could see which direction the 'friendly' hail was coming from, Jacob knew that it meant his best friend, actually his only friend, Neil was close by.

He was waiting in the car park of a biker bar called The Cat Dragged Inn on the lower east end of 3600 Street. This was also an informal meeting place for anyone who had something to sell that could not be advertised for sale by any of the conventional methods.

Crack, weed, crank, acid, heroin, uppers or downers, and a variety of stolen goods could be purchased here. Even the occasional hooker that was past her sell-by date, could be bought here, and usually for about the same price as a turkey club sandwich and a cup of coffee. Life was cheap in this part of town.

Out of the doorway of the Inn stepped the short rotund figure of Neil Whithers. Both he and Jacob had been loners all through high school, only associating with other teenagers if they had drugs to buy or sell, or knew someone who did. Theirs was a natural alliance, brought together initially by need, but becoming friends when realising that they shared the same interests, mainly that of getting wasted.

Following his usual greeting, which was responded to with a flippant, "Up yours," Neil got straight to the point.

"Have you sold that piece of crap stereo that we nicked yesterday?" he asked. "Cos with that money I can score for us big time tonight. How much did you get?"

It all came out in a garbled drunken torrent without him pausing for an answer to either question.

Jacob nodded yes.

"But, I only got forty bucks, so what's the big score you're on about, as you've never had one in your life."

Neil's flabby chest swelled with pride as if he was about to announce the winner of an Oscar award. His acne-scarred face beamed as he answered, "A full sheet of acid from fat Jessie. He's flat broke and desperately needs cash for his rent or something like that, but he needs it now."

A full sheet for forty dollars instead of the usual rate of eighty to a hundred was indeed a big score, and Jacob was secretly proud of his friends for such a prized commodity.

A full sheet to the A and E department of the local hospital however meant trouble. Usually a night of screaming students, who were experiencing something other than what they had expected.

An A4 size of old-fashioned blotting paper was impregnated with LSD; hopefully in a regular pattern. A single drop on every piece, about half the size of a postage stamp, would yield an average of over a hundred hits per sheet.

This would then be cut up into single pieces by the middleman, someone like Jacob, with each piece being sold for five dollars. The lucky user would quite simply chew and then swallow it. Moments later they would start to experience a whole new world.

However, all too often the pattern did not however go so uniformly regular as expected, meaning some poor dumb party freak would get a double or triple dose by mistake and end up shrieking his pathetic lungs out.

The hospital staff, although wanting to help, could do no more than strap the unfortunate individual up in a nice tight white jacket and place him or her in a secluded padded room. In there they could cry, screech, and rage until the effects wore off, hopefully without any long-term effects.

CHAPTER FOUR

Jacob didn't hesitate in handing the money to Neil, instructing him to, "Go and get it now before he changes his mind or finds another buyer, then meet me under the tree as soon as possible."

His subordinate friend left immediately, going as fast as his wobbly boozed and little body could walk.

Having about an hour to kill, Jacob wandered over to the nearby Burger King for a quick snack before heading up the hill to 'The tree.'

The meeting place he had instructed his partner in crime to meet him at was beneath an ancient majestic sycamore.

Standing over seventy feet tall and with branches spreading almost half that width, it was an impressive sight and the only dominant feature of Pioneer Park. In reality, the park was merely a field and not much else, and was directly adjacent to Salt Lake University, as such it was prime territory for plying their illegal trade.

Jacob and Neil's partnership could always be relied upon by some of the students requiring a little help during the stress of final exam times. Speed to keep them awake when cramming and downers to try and get some sleep when the exams were over. And, of course, a wide assortment of recreational drugs to be taken just for fun when boredom set in.

Students, not education were the only reason that Jacob ever regretted not going to university. If he had, it would have legitimised the reason for his frequent appearances on campus, and him not having to be constantly alert to the presence of the university police.

Jacob was surprised to discover that Neil was already waiting for him when he arrived at their designated meeting place. His friend hastily passed the prized paper to him.

"Catch you later," he said and hurriedly walked away.

Although he liked the money he received from their enterprise Neil did not relish the idea of spending several years in prison for dealing. That he would leave to his crony.

As discreetly as possible, Jacob took the innocuous-looking paper, folded it neatly into four, and then crammed it carelessly into the back pocket of his scruffy Levis.

Ragged jeans were not his fashion statement but were worn out of necessity. Expensive denims had always been difficult to steal due to the electronic tags so were, therefore, not worth the risk. Besides, there really wasn't anyone he needed to impress with his attire, and for the same cost as a new pair, he could buy enough beer and weed to stay high for several days. So, no contest.

He had decided to move his old Chevy further off campus, so as not to attract any unnecessary attention before looking for his regular customers. It was safer to select a new location for his recognisable car every time he visited the park as he did not want to become a familiar sight with the patrolling 'plastic police' as they were commonly referred to with distaste by most students. Besides, their jurisdiction exceeded the actual campus grounds by about half a mile.

Jacob chose to back the Impala into a space between a huge Dodge Ram pickup truck and a Conversion van. Here he was partially concealed and was confident that the car would not be seen with just a cursory glance by any patrols.

A newfound confidence filled him as he walked slowly back to his usual haunt looking as though he belonged there like any other student. About the same age, head down looking at their phones and oblivious of their surroundings, he fitted in perfectly.

Jacob could not even begin to guess how many hours he had spent sitting at the base of this wooden giant. Mostly sober, but more often drunk or high, he was always sharp enough to get the correct asking price for his wares.

The grass surrounding the tree had long since surrendered to the punishing summer sun. Despite the constant efforts of the automatic sprinkler system, it was now just coarse brown stubble. It was hard to the touch, even though it was soddened from its recent soaking.

The day began to heat up so Jacob removed his beloved leather bomber jacket, placing it behind his head to form a makeshift cushion.

The tree bark had almost completely worn away at this spot, due to the many visiting heads of students, and visitors, like Jacob, who favoured this particular place to relax or meet friends. The sycamore had become something of an old comfortable friend. One he did not have to participate in boring conversation with.

Although Jacob was without a formal education, he was not a stupid person. Uncouth, yes, self-centered and foul-mouthed, yes, but not without a certain knowledge that was self-taught.

When he was not drunk, high, or dealing with the reality of his miserable existence, he would read books. For the few people he associated with, it was always a surprise to discover that when he was lucid, his reading of choice included historical, scientific, and geographic volumes. This had also included research studies by the famous advocate of LSD use, none other than Professor Timothy Leary whose legacy was as dangerous as it was unpredictable.

During the 1960s and 1970s, and throughout the entire country, institutions for the criminally insane were home to many innocuous students and hippies who had never fully recovered from the use of this mind-altering hallucinogenic. The minority that had survived the unexpected and unwanted nightmares were still experiencing random flashbacks decades later.

Jacob's all-time favourite book, however, was by his hero, Aldous Leonard Huxley an English novelist. Huxley, who had been born in 1894, was a pioneer in the creative use of Mescalin (the forerunner to LSD). Both his grandfather and brother were renowned biologists and were the reason that Aldous became interested in this particular chemical. It was also known to be the principal active ingredient in the

Peyote cactus, used for many years by Native Americans in their 'vision quests.'

Aldous's most famous book, 'The Doors of Perception' had been written by him during his use of this powerful Hallucinogen. His tome had been widely accepted by many lost individuals seeking the knowledge of life and why we existed at all.

Strangely, one of Huxley's most famous devotees was the rock legend Jim Morrison, of whom there is a little-known fact that only those close to him were aware of.

Morrison was a shy man by nature, often turning his back on his adoring fans whilst performing. This he did not out of disdain, as some critics believed, or from attempting to look ultra cool, but rather out of sheer anxiety and panic. An audience of any size simply scared the poor man to death. In truth, Morrison had only ever wanted to be a poet and to perform his works, but this fear had always daunted his ambition.

That is, until one day when he came across the book that changed his life. Huxley believed that, 'several doors of awareness' existed, and that these could be opened by believers.

For those brave enough to try there was a door that showed us the world as we always wanted to see it. Another door as it truly is, and a third door into the unknown. Collectively they were called, 'The doors of perception.'

Jim Morrison, through his poetry and music, desperately wanted to be the means, by which we could all see this 'brave new world.'

Sadly he, and his band The Doors, were never to achieve this dream due to his untimely death.

CHAPTER FIVE

Jacob had fallen asleep leaning against his faithful old friend, his head tilted slightly to one side as he slumbered.

The tree was one of many that the hardy Mormon pioneers had planted many years ago. Not a native species to Utah they had been lovingly transported and cared for, to remind them of their original home. Now only the giant sycamore had survived the harsh punishing winters in the Rocky Mountains where they had established their community.

As Jacob dozed his thoughts wandered to memories of his old high school biology teacher, Mr. Adams, and what he had told his class about the structure of certain trees. Why some had roots that penetrated the soil and went almost vertically down into the earth to secure their survival during high winds. While others simply snaked along the surface of the ground as did this ancient one, before sinking their limbs into the security of softer soil.

Why this memory troubled Jacob was not yet apparent.

CHAPTER SIX

He woke abruptly, brought about by the sudden appearance of what he at first thought was the phenomenon known as the Northern Lights.

But he was bewildered as he knew it was the wrong time of year for the Aurora Borealis, and that Utah was too far south for them to be visible. That much he knew for sure. If not, the lights, he wondered, then what else was capable of such a breathtaking light show.

The answer to his unspoken questions was, sadly, in his back pocket. The grass, still slightly damp from its recent sprinkler soaking, had saturated his denim pockets. Subsequently, it had also seeped through to the all-important blotting paper.

As the paper became soggy, the acid permeated Jacob's jeans at an alarming rate. It was only a matter of about ten minutes before his frail body had soaked up enough of the drug to drive half a dozen adult males to the brink of permanent madness.

A once pale blue sky was rapidly becoming a curtain of mellow orange, yellow, and ochre. It pulsated slowly at first, before melting violently into a wave of menacing green, dark blue, and black. Colours that to Jacob's now unhinged mind could only have originated from the bowels of the earth.

They darted manically 'to-and-fro' in front of his transfixed eyes before exploding into a rainbow of a thousand colours, soon to be replaced by a blood-red heaven.

Then a moment of calmness enveloped him as a pale blue door slowly opened to allow a shimmering white beam of light to touch down at his feet. An ethereal female that was surely one of God's angels floated silently down the shaft towards him. Her voluptuous figure clad only in a diaphanous primrose-coloured sheet left no doubt as to her gender, or the perfection of her body.

Her pouting moist lips uttered not a single word, yet Jacob knew that she was asking him to come to her. The epitome of every young man's dream, all his fantasies rolled into this one beautiful Venus-like form. Without hesitation, he started to rise from his place beneath the tree but was perplexed when all his efforts could not budge his body a single inch.

He looked down to see that one of the smaller tree roots, which a moment ago had been content to spend its life laying across the surface of the loam, was moving. It was quietly wrapping its sinewy length around his left ankle before continuing to work itself even further up his entire leg.

More instinctively than out of fear Jacob abruptly pulled his leg upwards, and the timid root released its grip and retreated.

All that was beautiful and perfect only moments ago vanished. The light display was once again dark and menacing. Venus had disappeared. Worse was to follow.

Every single root of his beloved Sycamore was coming to life. The larger ones that supported the trunk began to shake themselves free, writhing as they did so. The smaller tubers only a few inches in diameter but over ten feet in length were squirming, forcing themselves up and out of their earthly prison.

Jacob noticed the fine hair-like fibres that normally absorbed the nutrition from the wet soil as they gleamed, struggling to adjust to their new life above ground.

Then the ends of smaller roots started to form some kind of head, similar to that of a venomous snake, but without any eyes. Using instead a foot-long thin forked tongue that was heat sensitive. That flicked from side to side in a rhythmic motion seeking out its prey.

The entire area around him was now undulating with the movement of what he was convinced were demons bent on his destruction. The once gentle giant, his friend and protection was giving birth to Satan's spores.

He felt himself urinating uncontrollably in his Levi's, his complete being trembling with terror.

'If I can only outrun the demonic roots,' he thought. 'Get back to my Chevy, I will be okay.'

With a final enormous effort, he jumped up, stumbled, but still managed to lurch forward and run blindly towards the parked car.

As he ran some of the smaller tubers broke free of the larger support limbs and formed into what something that resembled an angry centipede. Their tiny hairs had become legs, allowing them to propel themselves forward in a whip-like motion.

The tongues had disappeared, replaced by scores of minuscule razor-sharp teeth, capable of shredding the flesh of Jacob's legs in seconds.

An adrenaline-fueled burst of speed born out of self-preservation, drove Jacob onwards in seconds the last hundred feet to his car. Slamming the door shut, his hands shook as he rammed the key into the ignition. The engine purred immediately to life.

Dozens of those malevolent tormentors were surging towards the Chevy, his destruction their sole purpose in coming to life. The larger limbs had now joined in the hunt but were slower to move due to their sheer bulk.

He wanted to scream out loud but realised that terror had rendered him speechless.

Forcing the gearshift into first he sobbed silently as he floored the pedal. The speedometer displayed 60 MPH as he moved into third gear, then to 80 in fourth. His pursuers relentlessly continued the chase, visible in the rear-view mirror as the Chevy rocketed over the top of Chestnut Hill.

'If only I could outrun them and find somewhere safe to hide until they give up looking for me,' he thought.

A fuzzy memory unexpectedly emerged out of his subconscious mind and he knew where to find his best chance of survival.

Although still daylight, for some bizarre reason he knew that his tormentors would not be able to find him in the dark cavernous tunnel that he remembered lay at the bottom of the hill. Their powers he suspected existed only when powered by daylight. He could hide in the safety of the cavern until night time then make his way back to the car park of the Cat Dragged Inn where he was sure he would be safe.

A fleeting glance in the mirror told him his pursuers were steadily gaining on him, he had to go faster.

Jamming the pedal down as far as it would go, the needle jumped rapidly to its maximum position of 110 mph. Approaching the bottom of the hill at this speed he barely had time to read the sign that was posted at the entrance to the cave reading only the word, 'SAFE'.

The Chevy hurtled without hesitation into 'The cave.'

* * * * *

To the eyewitnesses who had read the entire message, it said, Safe and Secure Moving and Storage.

The 'cave' that Jacob had vaguely recalled on his way up the hill earlier that day was, in reality, a large black moving van.

The Mack truck that was barely two years old was now an almost unrecognisable heap of metal. The collision had pushed the three-ton vehicle over eighty feet further down the road, only coming to a stop when hitting a brick wall.

Amongst the metal, that was once a Chevy Impala, lay the unrecognisable body of Jacob Thompson. His life's blood having dripped slowly through the floor of the moving van before seeping into the earth.

The Sycamore centipedes momentarily lay caressingly on his body, and then they too slipped slowly into the soil, disappearing, forever.

THE DARKNESS OF DANIEL

Journeys of enjoyment are ones we return from.

It has been several months since my friend Daniel has passed away. Finally, I have finished dealing with the financial aspect of his estate, and I am now left with the unenviable task of making sense of the reams of notes he had accumulated during his lifetime.

I had always known him as an extremely sociable, positive although somewhat complex individual for most of his life, so was surprised and disturbed by what I was now reading.

There were his poems, dozens of unfinished stories, and several satirical Christmas songs; everything he had ever created but never shared with the world. They have left me with a sense of sadness, and yes, even a guilt that is difficult to explain. I am distraught at the dark and depressing thoughts that I only now realise must have tormented him these past twenty-odd years.

Throughout many of his papers, he expressed a feeling

of not being able to fit in at any level of society; or indeed in the culture of several of the countries, he had lived in.

'Where do I belong,' was written dozens of times in the margins of his papers. I could almost feel his anguish rising off the paper.

Reading this, I recall asking him a few years ago why, in all of the photographs I had seen of him, he never smiled. His answer had been simple, 'Because I have forgotten how to.'

It appears as though he spent many of the early morning hours trying to justify why he should even continue living. I know that he had a few friends like me, but sometimes I noticed the loneliness was seeping through the cracks of his public facade. He needed someone to watch his favourite movies with so he could share the funny parts he loved, or those that moved you to tears.

Only now do I understand how lonely and unhappy he was. He needed someone to share his life with.

I knew he would frantically write, often into the middle of the night, about what his mind had created; but I also knew how intensely he disliked the actual process of writing.

Once he had produced a story in its entirety in his mind;

the endless correcting and rewriting he only saw as a waste of time. I do not know if it was laziness on his part or the pure frustration of having to put down on paper what his mind had written out perfectly from beginning to end.

Either way, it was his dislike of this process that had led him to invent a computer program that he believed would relieve him of this tedium. It would, however, also lead to his eventual demise.

I know from our many conversations that Daniel had always been interested in practically all religions and ideologies. His thoughts and opinions ranged from an unquestionable belief in an omnipotent God, to theories on this same divine one being a visitor from an alien planet.

No matter which particular opinion I occasionally agreed with, he would then inevitably argue the opposing one convincingly. I have often wondered if perhaps I was sometimes a source of entertainment for him?

He was prone to throwing into the mix, that in his opinion, organised religion was the source of most of this world's evil. Never did I leave his company without some small doubt creeping into my own beliefs?

There were many occasions when Daniel, I, and a few selected acquaintances would dabble in the darker arts of the Ouija board. Often with many interesting, and dare I say sometimes frightening, unexplainable results from our futile attempts to determine if there was indeed an afterlife.

We all had the same questions.

'Are we reincarnated? Does life exist after death? Do we have a purpose?'

For those of us who participated in these sessions, it was fascinating, but for Daniel, it became an obsession.

Being an avid reader of all types of research on new uses for drugs, legal or otherwise, coupled with an interest in medical technology advances, he was steered towards what he theorised was the answer to his main objective.

He believed that it was possible to transfer his thoughts, and therefore his stories, directly to his computer printer. This would, in turn, leave him free to create without the tediousness of having to type!

His most recent scribbled, and almost indecipherable notes showed me that he had somehow obtained a variety of hallucinogenic drugs and opioids. Also, some electrical sensors that he would use to connect his brain directly to his computer.

To complicate me further, I must confess to never having had the need or desire to study the anatomy of neurology, so must admit that I was somewhat at a loss when attempting to understand the information I was looking at.

He wrote, that the 100 billion neurons within the brain that transmit messages to the specific lobes of the brain, both chemical and electrical signals, are used through the use of neurotransmitters. Any deviance in this process would affect the desired outcome. His studies included how these changes affected the personality of people with untreated and treated schizophrenia, and other mental health issues. He concluded that it was all due to this interruption of the neurotransmitter process.

Critically, what Daniel had focussed on was that artificial neural networks have been created by many scientists, and it was their studies that he had concentrated his work on. His theory was simple and, to my mind, even logical. With the correct hallucinogenic chemicals and other drugs, his brain would be able to convert his thoughts into electronic impulses and thus direct them to his computer printer.

There had followed months of what, I now read, were horrific experiments on himself until, eventually, he had achieved his goal.

However, this was not without some unforeseen consequences.

In my last few visits with him, I noticed that there were certain changes within his personality. He had become morose, often melancholy, saying how he had wasted many of the talents that he had been born with. And that, like many others before him, myself included, there was nothing to leave behind when he died. Nothing to show that he had accomplished anything of consequence. He could think of nothing worse than being simply... forgotten.

I had failed to connect these changing moods with his recent recurring obsession with the age-old question of whether there was life, of any kind, after death. Unknown to me, he had decided, that there was one earth-shattering achievement he could fulfil. One that would leave his mark on the history books. Something he would always be remembered for.

He had decided to use his creation to discover with

irrefutable proof that there was life after death. But, to do so it would mean that he would have to die.

It must have been during one of his darkest and anguished nights when he was just tired of life. Also possibly fuelled by too many glasses of gin and tonic, that he had decided it was time to put his theory to the test.

And so, wearing a crudely made cap to hold the sensors in place, he had carefully consumed measured amounts of chodonystatin,* orpthozaledine,* codoflaxcine,* and two hallucinogenics, the names of which were illegible. He had calculated that this combination would shut his body down quickly, yet still give his brain the several minutes of activity in which he could experience, and record what happens after you die. The printer would record not only his dying thoughts but would transmit what he saw of his existence after his physical death.

I now thank God that I was not the person who found him the next day; this, unfortunately, fell to the fate of his cleaning lady.

In her statement to the police, she said, "That she had found him leaning backward in his office chair; but, more upsetting than finding him dead was the look on his face."

The way she described him, it was as if his soul was being tortured. That his last few breaths had been tormented by whatever he was experiencing.

There was now only one final task that I had to perform to conclude my promised duties. I must examine the last few pages that had been printed out.

'Well, my friends, I have just taken the final step in this miserable existence, there is no going back. I believe that I am now officially deceased as I am unable to feel any parts of my body moving. Any moment now I am expecting my brain to shut down. I do not know whether this will happen instantly or slowly, but we shall soon know.'

The next page contained a series of jumbled letters and words which I find pointless in trying to decipher, but it continues with his last transmission; for want of a better description.

'I can no longer see anything that is in this room but, I feel a sense of peace, so think that I am now leaving this world, as my soul prepares to enter another dimension. There is a light that appears to be coming from a cone-shaped

tunnel, although it seems far away it appears quite bright. Too bright, almost blinding as I can see nothing else but that. I believe that I should now have some beautiful awareness of my soul leaving my body and entering the tunnel. My late family or ancestors will be greeting me soon, or even an angel guide.'

There was a foreboding, seemingly endless pause at this point, and then he continued.

'Something is happening, the light is dimming. It's gone, the tunnel has disappeared too. It's not supposed to be like this. It's getting darker, too dark. I don't like this, I expected something wonderful, not this. I don't like this at all. I am frightened now.'

'I seem to be losing control of my thoughts.' 'There is no one here for me, no one at all. Oh, ... dear God, I was wrong. It's just black now, nothing but pitch black, I cannot see, there is nothing, nothing, nothing, noth....'

As in his life, fate had dealt him one more cruel blow, as it was at this point that there had been an electric power failure. Only for a few minutes but enough to shut down his computer and printer.

Was there more? Did he find that there was an afterlife? Or was the blackness how it ended?

"Did you find the answerers you were looking for, Daniel?" I said aloud to his empty room, "Or did you just cease to exist?"

I sat on his sofa for one last time, wondering if I should share his story with the world.

I decided yes.

Although the proof of an afterlife would have sealed his place in history, his name will still be known. But, it will be known as the man who tried to answer the ultimate question and, although he failed, he gave his life in attempting to do so.

Leaving his home for the last time, I closed the door and quietly, said, "Goodbye, Daniel; wherever you are."

*** *Please note that the drugs named in this story - chodonystatin, orpthozaledine, and codoflaxcine, are all figments of the author's imagination and are not real drugs of any kind.*

MY BEST FRIEND

The closest I came to be with me?

I question myself. Do I believe in Karma? Or, if given the choice, would reincarnation be a better option for me, having to keep coming back until I get it right? Meaning, that one of these times I might just succeed, but this time wasn't going to be it.

Let me explain.

I was once married. However, I failed at that. I did, however, father two wonderful sons; the only thing in my life I can be proud of.

But, I also had numerous affairs; I suppose that speaks for itself. I even tried having a threesome - twice. Ha ha! Too confusing, and to be honest, certainly not worth the energy or the effort.

However, I believe I have been in love, I think, about nine times. Well, each time I believed I was. Predictably however, I was finally divorced.

Despite having that busy 'social life', I also somehow

managed to operate three nightclubs, a biker bar, and one restaurant, as well as somehow simultaneously finding the time to qualify as a counselling hypnotherapist.

Oh! And yes, I have also lived in and journeyed through, several different countries. So, it could be said that I have had an extremely busy life overall, one some people could call, 'a rich one'.

Which, I suppose, is a nice way, I believe, of them saying I am, 'extremely dysfunctional.'

And yet, I have always felt unfulfilled in everything that I have done.

I was never satisfied, and to be frank, most of the time, I was not always happy either, or even mildly contented. There has been this feeling of always searching for something; as if there was a large part of me that knew something was missing in my life, even though I didn't know what that was.

Although I travelled far and wide, I never really felt I belonged in any of the towns or countries I temporarily settled in.

So, this has left me wondering, if it now makes a difference, at this point in my life, as to whether or not I should worry about where I want to spend the rest of my days. After all, I have only ever known the urge for, once again, needing to seek out new pastures, with the hope of discovering where I truly belong.

I have always been a believer in the old adage, "You can never go home again," and yet, 28 years later, I still find myself single, living in a small but comfortable apartment, only a few miles from where I was born and raised.

For a long time, I felt like a stranger, a foreigner in the country of my birth. No longer did I have anything in common with the people I had grown up with.

That caused me to question, 'Had I, yet again, made another gigantic mistake? Would I once more soon be thinking about moving on?

But it was here that I found the one thing that I had unknowingly been searching for all my adult life. The one thing I had been missing.

My best friend and, for those of us who believe in it, my soul mate.

Could it be merely a coincidence she lived only a few doors away from my new home?

My attraction was, at first, typical of my shallowness. She was extremely attractive, had a beautiful heartwarming smile, a good figure, was intelligent, and displayed an engaging personality.

Astonishingly, she was immediately attracted to me. And almost overnight, our fledgling relationship developed from something uncomplicated into our becoming lovers. Although, surprisingly, this part of our relationship only lasted for a short time.

No conscious decisions were made, and no conversations were held. There was something about our feelings for each other that meant we no longer needed a physical relationship. This in itself was alien to me considering my past behaviour.

And yet, it was as if we did not want to harm what we felt for each other. Instead, simply being in each other's company as often as possible, seemed to satisfy whatever one human being wants from another.

Although we still lived in our individual apartments, we were otherwise inseparable.

Not a day would pass without us seeing each other. All shopping had to be done together. Medical appointments, optician appointments, and even Dental were all made but only if we were able to accompany each other for support, or simply just for the company.

In some respects, we appeared to be like an old married couple. Even our neighbours would often say how we were joined at the hip other than us living in our respective homes.

I constantly reflect on the twenty years we knew each other, and think that yes, **we** had become a big part of each other's lives. But it is only now that I realise how it was so much more than that, much, much more.

She had not only become a huge part of my life. She was the part of me I had been missing. What I had unknowingly been searching for. Finally, I felt happy and complete.

So, do I have any regrets?

Absolutely. Yes I do. And yet there is one in particular that will always haunt me.

We had been on an out-of-town shopping expedition and were returning home in heavy traffic. This required my constantly changing gears so I was grumbling, saying, "My next car is going to be an automatic."

My hand was on the gearshift once more when I felt her

hand gently placed on top of mine. Looking at me, she smiled, and quietly said, "I love you."

To this day I have no idea why I did not respond.

Was it some subconscious leftover juvenile fear of commitment, or just the surprise of the unexpected?

I know not.

I just simply smiled at her.

We had never talked about love. Why, I don't really know. There just never seemed to be the need to. We were as close as two people could ever be and yet, that day, I did not respond.

Sadly, never again was she to tell me she loved me. And yet, our relationship did continue as normal.

I had known for many years that she suffered from several illnesses, although she never complained. Some were mild, being controlled by medication, whilst others quickly became more serious.

It was the latter that caused me to be late home one evening, after my insisting I take her to the hospital. Following an examination she had been immediately admitted.

For six weeks, I continued to see her every day, except at weekends when her family visited.

I was therefore, surprised, when on a Saturday evening she called me, asking if I going to visit her the next day, once her family had left.

Casually, I had replied, "No. I will see you Monday as usual."

Sadly, this was not to be, as overnight, while I slept soundly in my bed, this beautiful loving soul suddenly succumbed to her illness. The only shining light in my life was cruelly and prematurely extinguished.

"Has she phoned asking me to visit as she had some kind of premonition of her imminent departure from this planet?"

I know not.

Was I so lacking in empathy? So ignorant that I could not see that she wanted me to be with her? That she needed me to be there?

I still know not.

But, it is something that I have regretfully wrestled with

every day since.

The clothes I collected from her home, to be worn when I anticipated her discharge from the hospital, still hang on the door of my closet. Never to be worn, they are a daily reminder of my remorse.

Throughout my life, I have often heard people say, "You don't know what you are missing until it's gone."

Never have truer words been spoken, and are the ones I now live with every day.

Was she the soul mate that I unknowingly spent my life searching for?

Definitely.

Was she the best friend I have ever had in my entire life?

OH, Yes.

Will anyone ever be able to replace her?

No.

Only now, do I understand why, when I had that one chance, I should have simply replied, "And, I love you, too."

GOING HOME

There is more to this world than we know.

"Hello, Mum, how are you feeling today?"

Letitia looked up from the hospital bed at her only daughter.

"Well now, Caroline, let me see! I am ninety-six years old and am lying here in a palliative care ward. Today, I am surrounded by most of our relatives, many of whom haven't visited me for a very long time, therefore, I must assume that means I am dying."

"So, considering all of that, and in answer to your question, I really don't feel too bad," she answered with a wry smile that was typical of her sense of humour.

Letitia's tiny frame looked even smaller now than when she had been a young woman. Even then she was, at most, five-foot one inch tall. But, what she had lacked in stature she had made up for in her strength of spirit, being known as a woman who could always be relied upon for help, when and if needed.

Her family smiled sheepishly, with several of them feeling slightly guilty, yet all remained silent. Not one of them knew how to respond to her blunt but honest answer.

She waited patiently for some kind of utterance of remorse from the gathered relatives. With none forthcoming, she spoke again.

"I think I am now ready to leave this life and, to be quite truthful with all of you, I am at peace with myself. I know that I have been a good person, having raised my children lovingly, and to the best of my ability."

"I am also sure, that if the tunnel of light that I have heard about for so many years truly exists, then my mother, father, and my loving husband will all be waiting at the end of it to greet me."

No-one spoke.

Once the obligatory time of attendance had passed, the relatives slowly filtered out of the room, until the last, most loyal of her children was left. Her daughter Caroline.

Gently, Letitia said, "You must leave too; I need to be on my own now."

Caroline bent down and kissed her mother on the cheek. She smiled at her, knowing what was being implied before she too reluctantly left the room.

At last, Letitia finally on her own, was able to reflect upon her life.

'I have so many fond memories,' she thought. 'Most are of my children and my husband. Of how we sometimes struggled financially at the end of the Second World War. Mind you, we always made sure the children were well fed and clothed, even if we sometimes had to make sacrifices ourselves.'

Closing her eyes, she fondly remembered her husband, Melfyn. Upon returning home from fighting in the war, and despite being worn out he immediately sought out some work to provide for his family.

"They don't make men like him anymore," mused Letitia sighing softly.

"I believe I have done all I can as a mother and I'm ready to leave this life. God willing, there will be a light at the end of the tunnel, and I will meet every one of my long-deceased relatives and good friends."

Later that night, Letitia peacefully passed away. As expected, her soul slowly separated from her now tired and lifeless body and she did indeed go into a tunnel of light.

* * * * *

After Letitia had entered the light, there had followed a brief amount of time, during which she had felt confused by all the thoughts that were going through her disembodied mind. Peculiar faint memories were mixed with anxiety, but also with peace. Almost as if every emotion imaginable was being experienced in what was only a matter of a few seconds.

Finally emerging from the tunnel Letitia, just as she had hoped, was soon greeted by several family members. Although there were many others there whom she did not recognise.

"Is this heaven?" she asked of no one in particular. "It does not look anything like what I had imagined it to be, and I did not expect to see so many people, especially in the physical form."

All at once a tall distinguished male figure came forward and introduced himself.

"Hello, Letitia. I am Elam and I have been assigned to welcome you. I know that this feeling is very unfamiliar to you at the moment and that it will take you some time to adjust to what you are seeing and what you will hear. But do not worry."

He paused to allow her to assess his words. Then he continued speaking.

"You have been in your earthly body, this time, for almost one hundred years. Who you truly are and where you come from is, understandably, no more than a tiny glimmer somewhere in your memory. But, that too will change." And he smiled warmly.

"I think it best for now that you meet with those you hoped to find waiting here. They will help explain to you what this 'heaven' actually is."

Letitia soon found herself surrounded by people who had loved and missed her. However, she was especially delighted to see her husband, Melfyn, standing in front of her. They hugged each other tightly. Neither spoke, as the bond of love between them had been formed many years ago when they had first met. For them words were unnecessary. It was as if no time at all had passed since they had last been together, and yet it had been almost ten years since he had shed his earthly body.

Slowly, she was beginning to accept that she was not in any kind of spirit or energy form as she had always thought she would be. Somehow, she had acquired a physical body, similar to the one she had before her passing. However, this one was younger and more beautiful; much the same as the one she remembered having from her early womanhood.

After a brief time of being welcomed by all those who knew her, Melfyn steered her away to a quiet place where they could sit and talk. Letitia held his hand tightly, as if letting go would cause her to lose him once again.

Her husband smiled, "I know that this is not what you were expecting heaven to be like. You often told me that it would be full of beautiful fields of flowers, with all kinds of animals running free, like those you used to read about in the children's storybooks. But, my love, this is where you came from, and soon you and I will finally be going home."

Letitia looked around as Melfyn spoke. She appeared to be sitting in a vast enclosed auditorium of some kind, so large, that where it began or ended was impossible to see. Windows surrounded the entire area so no matter where you looked a view of the heavens was visible. And, although the light did not hurt her eyes, the whole interior seemed to glow with a white light that she found inexplicably comforting.

Sensing her bewilderment her husband held her even closer to him, as he explained. "Where we are sitting at this moment is what people on earth in science fiction stories and movies would call a Mother Ship, which is certainly a pretty accurate definition of it. There are many similar crafts to this one scattered throughout the outer atmosphere of Earth but in a parallel universe. They have been a temporary home to all of us who waited a little while longer for all of our people to return."

Letitia interrupted, saying hesitantly, "I seem to have faint memories returning to me, but I would prefer it if you would explain everything. Besides, I love hearing your voice again."

Melfyn smiled and continued. "Many thousands of years ago, everyone that is on this ship, including us, were part of an exploratory mission to find a particular type of planet."

Letitia laughed, interrupting again, "Sorry, Melfyn, but am I actually that old?"

Her husband nodded yes, smiling at his wife, before continuing.

"Our home planet was just like Earth is now. The atmosphere was getting thinner from the harmful penetrating rays of our sun, which was heating the oceans and killing all marine life. The lush agricultural land became too dry to grow crops, so firestorms became commonplace. Soon it started to grow warmer with every passing year."

He paused for a moment, then went on. "Eventually, our climate scientists announced that within only a few decades the world we lived on would no longer be habitable, having been reduced to a hot arid wasteland."

Here Melfyn paused again, then he said, "I think the next piece of information is best left to Elam to explain for he has a better understanding of the science than I do."

At this point, Elam, who had been standing close by listening, immediately came across as Melfyn beckoned him to answer.

As a science officer, Elam was a fountain of knowledge.

He began by explaining how the only chance of survival had been to surround their entire planet's atmosphere in vast quantities of gold dust. This would break up the reflecting heat rays coming from our sun, diverting them away from the planet.

He paused, as he could see that Letitia was anxious to ask him a question.

"Why gold dust? I don't understand," she asked with a frown.

Elam articulately replied, "Because gold is an ideal conductor of electricity, and therefore a perfect reflector of infrared energy. This is also why this craft has a thin coating of gold all over it. That way we are protected against any intense heat if we should stray too near to a star or another galaxy's sun."

Letitia thanked him for his explanation and asked him to please carry on.

"Could our world be saved? Yes, but there was a problem with this concept. There simply wasn't enough gold deposits available on our planet to achieve this goal. Consequently, a decision was made that every available mothership, like this one, would go out and search for parallel universes. It was hoped that a planet would be discovered where gold could be found in the quantities that we so desperately needed."

"And did they?" asked Letitia.

"Fortunately, yes they did. In a few short years, Earth was discovered, and messages were transmitted to all the other crafts to congregate here and begin the process of mining the needed precious metal. However, there remained one big problem," said Elam. "Even if every crew member of every ship worked in the mining process, there still might not be enough time left to save our world. Therefore, we could see only one answer to resolve this."

Elam stopped speaking, and looking at Letitia, he said, "Before I continue as to how that was resolved, let me explain some of your stored memories and the belief in what heaven would look like for you."

Letitia smiled and nodded, for she was truly interested in whether or not God and heaven existed. If it didn't, then what would replace it?

Elam began explaining.

"When we all first arrived, planet Earth looked just as your description of what heaven should look like. It was a beautiful and wonderous place. All the land was covered in green fields full of flowers and plants. Tall trees were home to many kinds of birds and small mammals. Strange large animals roamed the vast plains. There were mountains capped with snow and oceans that were crystal clear and cool."

Elam stopped talking. He was silent for a moment. As if he was remembering the Earth he had first visited.

"It was what paradise should look like," he went on. "This is what you experienced when you first came here, and for you, that became a distant memory. This is what you came to believe heaven looks like."

Letitia smiled as she recalled the memory, but Elam disturbed her thoughts as he went on.

"But, to return to how the problem was solved. A meeting of senior advisors was hurriedly convened, on this very ship. After much debate, and regardless of the potential consequences of doing so, it was decided there was only one way to solve the workforce problem. We had to create another life form, and that became - mankind. We needed to ensure that they would be created in our image, so clones were reproduced of every single crew member, from every ship. They were then put to work alongside their creators."

"Wow," was all Letitia could say.

"Yes," smiled Elam agreeing. "Wow, certainly says it all.

Anyway, eventually enough of the precious metal we required was gathered and finally, plans were made to return home, hopefully in time to save our planet. But, before we left, it was suggested, that although our clones could survive for many years without our presence, they should be rewarded for their tireless labours. And so, they were given the gift of a soul - just like ours."

Merflyn nodded his head, saying, "And that is where religion came from, wasn't it? The belief in souls?"

"Probably," agreed Elam. "However, it was felt, that as long as they did not disgrace their soul, when their mortal body aged and eventually died, they would be able to be reborn into a new body, again and again, just as we are."

Letitia frowned, and wondering she asked, "Will I change into someone new?"

"Let me explain further," said Elam, "The soul was created out of love, so if the body which it inhabits should become someone who develops undesirable traits, then the soul would leave them immediately. At the end of their natural cycle of life, they would return to dust, meaning they would simply cease to exist.

It was now that Melfyn interrupted Elam, saying. "I think you should also explain how they were given this gift, and what a soul actually is, so Letitia has a better understanding."

"Yes, of course," Elam replied. "Letitia, it is a simple but beautiful process. A soul is made up of a very specific type of energy, or essence but, it is only half of what is called a twin flame, or mirror soul. When two people love each other deeply, they are able to combine both these halves, thus creating a complete soul. Between them, they ignite this spark of life, thus becoming one that cannot manifest itself physically."

"Therefore, it becomes an entity that exists as a powerful life form of its own. But, being made of love it needs to exist in a body that accepts its love, and will continue forever to heal, giving life to the physical form that it occupies."

"Mmm... I think I understand," said Letitia a little hesitantly.

"Let me try to make it a little clearer. When you returned to us through the tunnel of light, which is essentially a regenerative process, by the time you emerged you had already been reincarnated," Elam told her. "With the memory of your past lives on earth slowly beginning to return to you.

However, your time on this planet, like millions of others, must now come to an end."

"But why now, after all these years?" Letitia asked.

Patiently, Elam went on. "After the successful deployment of the gold dust in our atmosphere, we felt it a duty to periodically return to earth and ensure that life continued the way we expected it to."

At this point, Elam's demeanour changed and his face betrayed a heart- rendering sadness. Sighing, he carried on talking.

"However, what we have discovered, on this our last visit, is worse than any one of us could ever have imagined. Where we expected to see thriving happy communities, we have found starvation and disease. Instead of harmony, mankind has scattered to the various parts of the planet and are now killing each other. They are fighting over land and natural resources. Nations have been formed and wars fought for reasons that are beyond even my comprehension."

Elam paused as the memories of what he had seen disturbed him. Then he continued.

"Neighbours are jealous of each other's insignificant

possessions and will steal from one another. Innocent animals are being slaughtered and eaten, or used as bloodthirsty sacrifices to imaginary gods. They are even killing, simply for what they call sport."

"Religions were created, with hostility between them now being commonplace, usually over whose religion is the true one. Ironically many religious wars were waged, killing each other to decide who was the more peace-loving one. Greed and power have become the norm. Individuals' wants and desires mean more than what is best for humanity. But, the most distressing of anything we have so far witnessed is what has been done to the planet."

And here Elam had to stop and take a deep breath before continuing.

"I do not need to tell you everything that has sickened us, as you have been witness to most of it in your last few lives. You too will have seen the destruction caused by climate change. The pollution of the oceans, and the destruction of the forests and the animals' habitats. Firestorms and floods, extreme temperatures, and food shortages There is an endless list of devastation."

"But, now it is as if the planet is trying to fight back,

trying to save itself. The mankind we created has now become abhorrent to us, being a selfish and self- destructive creature, an abomination."

"I think it only right to mention, that there have been individuals such as naturalists, climate scientists, and just ordinary people who have made it their mortal lives work to try and educate people," Melfyn reminded Elam.

"Yes, that is true, I will admit that," replied Elam, "but, even when these warnings were heeded by some, others again found ways to use it for their own avaricious gain."

And once more he paused, before saying, "Consider just one example of this. Replacing car engines that once used fossil fuels with electric power was one idea to reduce carbon dioxide levels. Yet, this positive has been defeated by the necessity of these machines requiring huge batteries to operate efficiently. In creating these batteries it has subsequently meant intensive mining of vast quantities of minerals such as Manganese, Cobalt, and Lithium. And this mining process has caused more environmental damage than fossil fuels ever have. Yet, that fact has been deliberately ignored as too much money is being generated by this 'environmental saviour,'" said Elam cynically.

Elam looked as if he wanted to throw up, so disgusted was he at the waste and devastation of the beautiful planet he had once loved so dearly.

Controlling his temper and feelings, he continued explaining.

"Equally inexcusable are the huge companies and the large number of countries whose intent it is in ravishing the floors of the oceans to extract these minerals. Which, of course, has caused further pollution of the oceans and the death of most of the remaining marine life."

Letitia nodded her head in agreement. She remembered how much pleasure she had once gotten from taking the children to the seaside so they could play on the beach and swim in the sea. Then she recalled how eventually her daughter, Caroline, had refused to go because the sea was full of plastics and sewage, and how it now wasn't safe for the kids to swim in it.

Merfyn said, "Sometimes it is difficult to separate man's egocentric greed from his stupidity."

Nodding his head, Elam went on. "When we returned to earth this last time, we were inundated with souls that had removed themselves from their host bodies, as they wanted to reintegrate with their creator couple. So many, that we signalled for all the original craft and their crews to return here immediately. We cannot tell what the future of Earth will be. But, what is irrefutable, is that within a very short period of time, and due to either nuclear wars, irreversible global warming, or natural or man-made disasters this world is doomed. Even the possibility of interference by Artificial Intelligence, or one of the many other probabilities cannot and will not stop the destruction."

"What does this mean for our children?" asked Letitia worried.

Looking at her, Elam sadly said, "I am not sure. The planet Earth that you have lived on, that was your home for countless numbers of your lives, will cease to exist as a habitable one. You, and millions like you, who have returned to us through the tunnel of light must now prepare for the journey to our home planet."

"Yes, there are many of us with pure unblemished souls, who might insist on remaining here. Perhaps, they will continue to hope, while searching for solutions that could save Earth but," and here he sighed, "that is their choice."

Letitia and Melvyn looked at each other with happiness, yet both were still filled with a sense of sadness at the loss of their children.

Finally, Elam concluded, "And yes, there is always hope. Although that window of opportunity is getting smaller every day. However, for us our time here has come to an end. Possibly we may return in the distant future when, hopefully, there may still be some signs of life here. Until then, there is nothing more that we can do."

Then standing, he instructed the couple, "Come, we only have a short time left before the last of our people will have finished returning through the tunnel, then Letitia, we will all go home. I cannot say what will come of your family but, I believe, that if mankind is to survive it is now entirely up to them and all those like-minded souls."

The End

... or is it?

THE FAT LADY IS SINGING

It isn't over just yet – is it?

This is the first entry in a journal that will document the beginning of a new, but also the final chapter of my life.

My name is Henry Long, and tomorrow, the 28th of September 2047, is my seventieth birthday. My son and his family will, hopefully, be able to visit me. I am of course anxiously looking forward to seeing them.

However, it will also be the last time we see each other until my next birthday, as on the 29th I will be moving from my current home to UK Region Twelve; the same as many others my age who have miraculously survived the past decade, have done. I will be collected by someone from one of the relocation agencies and taken to my new home.

I will explain later in this journal why this is necessary.

The new accommodation provided will, I have no doubt, meet the basic requirements for senior citizens as agreed and established by the national security federation.

However, I remember a very old television sitcom where the presenter pointed to a large block of flats, humorously saying, "And this is where we store our old people."

Unfortunately, this has now become a frightening reality.

Sometimes, I sit back and reflect on how we, a so-called civilised society, have arrived at the situation our planet is now in. Long ago, I concluded that we were never actually civilized at all. We simply progressed. Driven forward by our petty wants and imagined needs.

It was over thirty years ago that several popular, educated, and supposedly well-informed individuals, had tried desperately for most of their lives to make the world aware of the self-destructive path we had made for ourselves.

Publicly they were applauded, being lavishly praised by mainstream media and governments alike. Yet, in reality, they were ignored whilst our lives carried on as normal, at least for a while.

Often I find myself laughing quietly at some of the past news programs, proudly announcing that after years of intense study, governments were making it illegal to provide and use plastic disposable shopping bags. Sadly this seemed to appease the general public, who believed that doing this would help solve all our entire environmental problems.

Really? Were we that stupid and gullible? Yes, I am afraid we were.

I try with great difficulty not to reflect on the past, but I do try to recall all I can, recording it here. I do not want our grandchildren to be misled into thinking that they were in any way able to prevent the destruction of society as it was and eventually our planet. It is solely the fault of my generation, plus some of those before us.

It would be wrong of me to pinpoint a specific individual, company, or government as being the sole cause. No, rather it was a tsunami of global events. Irreversible climate change was upon us. We had gone too far. Way past the point of return.

We had become a society that believed it was our right to have anything we wanted, and when we wanted it.

We also became lazy consumers. At the push of a few buttons, our cravings were delivered overnight to our doorstep. No thought being given to the origin or construction of our purchase, or indeed the environmental damage its production may have caused.

Major appliances were made to be obsolete within five years, with only some parts being recyclable. The rest was added to the landfill sites. The water and air pollution generated by the manufacture of products, clothing, etc., was something we did not even consider, or worse, even care about. And yet, we gaily ploughed on.

Countries that were once considered poor, become wealthy practically overnight, due to their cheap labour force, who had total disregard for any environmental dangers.

Thousands of factories polluted the rivers and oceans with their poisonous by-products. I recall with sadness a video taken in an Asian country, showing trucks lining up on a dock waiting to dump all their toxic garbage directly into the ocean. One I had once swum in, commenting how beautiful and clear it had been at the time.

Air quality became noxious, with our having to wear masks, in order to prevent lung damage.

Warnings of climate change were continually rejected, even ridiculed, until eventually they could no longer be ignored. The Antarctic ice sheet melted faster than even scientists thought was possible. Causing sea levels to rise, and coastal cities around the world to be submerged.

By this time, the pollution and dramatic changes in the weather patterns were causing a myriad of disasters.

Floods, landslides, earthquakes, and typhoons were becoming commonplace. Wildfires, which previously had only happened during the summer months, were now a regular occurrence, often scorching thousands of square miles of land and destroying wildlife on every continent. Extreme weather was commonplace and unpredictable.

Yet, billions were poured into the continuation of space exploration. Why didn't they realise that the money could have helped save us and our planet.

I thought at first it was a search for another planet that we could inhabit, but eventually, the real reason surfaced. Mars, thought to be our new home once the destruction of this one became inevitable was, in reality, only investigated for the sole purpose of mining its minerals. Ones in short supply here and that were needed in the manufacture of many of our consumer goods. Unbelievably, amid the problems facing us, the need to produce consumer goods was still paramount.

I should mention that my timeline of events is not necessarily in the correct order as many may have overlapped. It is only important to note that they have happened.

Ironically, many of the industrial leaders that were complicit in establishing our progressive society, were now being consulted by our governments for help to solve some of the problems they helped create.

I don't know if you have ever read the definition of a Technocrat or Megalomaniac, but the former is a person who is a technical expert, wielding great power and influence within both industry and governments.

The latter, the Megalomaniac, is probably the most scariest to me. The ones who have the drive to control people have a sense of greatness by believing they are omnipotent. Strangely this was once classed as a severe mental illness. Yet, it was to these individuals that we turned for help.

Think, isn't that like having the fox guarding the henhouse?

Oceans, so full of plastic combined with an increase in water temperature, killed most of the marine life. Once fertile soil dried up into barren wastelands. Animals died due to a lack of vegetation, drinking water, and extreme heat. Food for man and beast alike became scarce. Entire nations on several continents died of starvation.

And, as if these disasters were not enough to cope with, very few countries escaped the emerging new plague-like viruses. The origins of which I am unsure. Natural, manmade, or perhaps both? There was too much misinformation for me to speculate on the true source, although I do have my suspicions.

And yet we still ploughed on.

Within only a decade, the planet's population was reduced to about two billion souls!

There were, of course, pockets of civilization that survived. Parts of the UK, New Zealand, Iceland, the central plains of America, plus a few remote small islands. It was these countries that, for a brief time, were to experience the mass migration of refugees.

Sadly, many of those landing on coastal areas were met by hostile vigilante groups that repelled their attempts to reach land. Most were seen as invaders, not refugees.

Extreme violence now seemed to be acceptable, often being used by the self-appointed guardians of their homelands. Humanity no longer had a place in the tattered remains of society.

With only makeshift governments now in existence, numerous attempts were made to try and hold society together.

They all failed.

The introduction of digital currency, when other forms crashed, also failed.

The introduction of a wearable biometric device that monitored your health, but also gathered your security risk and status, failed. For most of the planet, the societal collapse was complete.

With employment scarce, there was little in the way of taxes to be collected. No money to pay for services, of course, meant no police force, no fire department, no health service, and no public transport.

The only transport available was used by the few volunteer civil servants who serviced the housing blocks. This transport was unreliable too as the electric cars, now the only type to exist had to rely on a very unpredictable national power grid. Wind farms and solar panels were at the mercy of extreme weather, so most times, they could not provide enough electricity to charge these few remaining vehicles.

The majority of people that did survive moved to rural areas where they were able to grow a few meagre crops to support themselves. The barter system surfaced once again, replacing currency. And old people like me were transferred to central blocks of housing, where we had some minimal form of protection and help, as crime became epidemic. Once tight communities no longer existed. We were now living in a 'dog eat dog' world.

Amazingly, considering the apocalyptic situation we now found ourselves in, there were still large, once-powerful countries run by dictators, plus a few small ones, ready to start international wars. Some were even using nuclear weapons, in the misguided and desperate attempts, to survive. Not only was this a wanton destruction of more human life but also resulted in vast amounts of land made uninhabitable for thousands of years to come.

Two of these warlike nations were so vast that their population only inhabited a comparatively small portion of their country anyway. I have never been able to comprehend the insane desire to continually expand your country's borders when you had more land than you could ever possibly need.

Yet still, we ploughed on.

For a brief period, there was a renewed belief in religion. Desperate for help, people prayed to the gods of various faiths. But, when no relief came, only a minority of fanatics continued to believe that God would return to save us.

I know that I have not recorded all I should, but my memory is not as sharp as it used to be. Still, I hope I have written enough for you to consider where you went wrong.

I will finish writing for now as I have to pack my few belongings in preparation for my move.

However, I will leave you with my final thoughts.

Race, religion, and the colour of our skin should not separate us. We are all the same species. We should all care about each other. We are each other's caretakers and the caretakers of this planet we were given. I cannot remember where I heard this phrase, maybe from an old song? But, now it has a more appropriate meaning to me than when I first heard it, 'United we stand, divided we fall.' So, I say, unite, grow stronger, love one another, and for God's sake, learn from our mistakes, mine included.

After my family leaves tomorrow and I am relocated to my new home, I will continue to write more for history's sake. I think I need a heading for part two of the journal.

Maybe I should call it, 'And yet we ploughed on!' Let's hope we survived.

HEART

The innermost part of something.

I am probably the only person in the world who would say they were so lucky to have had a heart attack.

Although, I think that statement needs some explanation. I think it was more a case of how fortunate I was to be where I was when I felt the first symptoms.

I remember sitting in the waiting room of my local hospital for a routine exam with an Audiologist when a feeling of anxiety suddenly swept over me. For no reason that made any sense to me, I began to perspire. Then, only moments later, I started to experience a tightness in my chest which quickly got worse, until it felt as if someone was not just sitting on my chest, but was pushing down on it, as if they were trying to prevent me from breathing.

As if that wasn't enough, a dull pain in my arm and shoulder suddenly caused me to involuntary gasp out loud, bringing attention to everyone in my immediate vicinity. I soon lost consciousness, aware of nothing, until I woke up sometime later, feeling drowsy but safe in a hospital bed, remembering nothing of what had happened.

To be truthful there was little I could accurately recall from that time until now as I write this narrative.

I was told that, as is normal procedure, my next of kin were called, being informed that my heart had, to simply put it, become worn out. And, if I was to have any chance of survival I would need an immediate heart transplant. That is, if a suitable donor could be located in time. They had, of course, agreed, giving the appropriate permission for this to happen.

To say I was blessed sounds cold and callous, as it was only through the untimely passing of another soul that my life was to be saved. And as it happened a man had recently passed.

He had been about my age, in his early forties and thus it was he who became my life- saving donor.

As is normal all the important decisions were made and quickly acted upon while I was still in a sedated condition. Not having enough awareness to understand that I was about to undergo immediate surgery.

Needless to say, the operation was successful, and once I regained consciousness, I eventually discovered that I was still alive, albeit while only in a partly lucid condition.

Yet, even in this semi-dozy state, I felt uneasy about

something. Something that I could not quite put my finger on. This becoming more obvious once I had returned home having been discharged into the care of my family.

For some inexplicable reason, I felt different!

Oh, I was happy to be alive but, I was still settled with an uneasy feeling that I could not, at first, understand. However, in time I did.

The feeling was that I was missing my heart.

Yes, of course, I know I now had a new one. And that I had another chance at life. But, this new heart was not mine. The one I had been born with. The one I had used all these years.

I had always known the importance of which part of our brain was responsible for everything that we do; our movements, taste, touch, logic, etc., and in particular, about how the temporal lobe processes and contains our memories.

But, there have also been studies that prove the heart also receives and transmits messages and emotions, and this is what I know to be a scientific fact.

Why else would there be expressions such as being heartbroken, heartfelt, a heart full of love, she/he captured my heart and many more?

My heart, my first heart, had contained all of my loves

and passions.

My deepest and fondest memories.

Everything that I was.

It was me, and they just… threw it away. Discarding it as if it was a piece of bad meat.

Yet, it wasn't.

It had been full of love, compassion, fond recollections, nostalgia, secrets and desires, passions, everything that had made me what I once was.

It had contained what was the most beautiful part of me, but now it was gone.

Everything that I had been, now no longer existed.

Besides, neither did I believe, that it had just gotten worn out.

No.

It was like the memory drive on the laptop; it had just got a little… too full.

I also knew nothing about the person whose heart now occupied my body; other than his age. And that medically it was a perfect match.

But… it had also been used.

The question is, had it been used as much as mine had?

Had it experienced a full life just as mine had?

Had they emptied it before putting it inside me?

Had his departing soul taken all of his memories and emotions with him? Or did he leave them for me to discover?

Is it truly empty or is there only just enough room for a few memories?

Or, is it just beating, waiting for me to replace them with new memories of my own?

There are no answers.

So I suppose only time will tell.

THE LONELIEST CHRISTMAS

A moment of joy and wonder!

It was going to be another lonely Christmas for Ann. The snow had been falling almost nonstop for nearly three weeks, with the drifts piled high against the few houses that made this mountain area home. It was now almost impossible to even push open the front door.

Fortunately, she had foreseen the possibility of becoming housebound as she recalled the great winter of thirty years ago when it had snowed heavily from December until March. And so, at the first sign of another harsh winter, she had made sure to buy enough food and provisions to last her and her dog Cleo, until early spring.

Winter months were often cold and windy in this remote part of Wales, and although her few neighbours were friendly, it was sometimes weeks before they were able to call on each other.

Today was Christmas Eve. On this day, over the past many years, she would usually visit one of her neighbours, spending a few pleasant hours, talking, eating mince pies, and simply enjoying their company.

However, the heavy snowfall this year had made that impossible. To even venture just outside her door to bring in firewood was difficult enough, so trying to walk any further than that would have been reckless and foolish.

Thus, Ann had reconciled herself to the fact that she would be spending Christmas on her own; except of course for Cleo.

Putting enough wood on the fire to last the rest of the evening, she made a large mug of hot coffee before settling herself in the armchair by the fireplace. She also didn't forget a nice snack for Cleo to enjoy, who now lay in the warmth coming from the log fire.

Although Ann was content with her solitary lifestyle, the enforced confinement gave her many hours to reflect on her life. Time from when she was a young girl - to now as an old woman. The memories soon came flooding back.

Most times there were happy thoughts, but tonight she gripped her mug tightly as she recalled with sadness some of the events of her younger days.

Sometimes, she thought it was best not to think of the past, but tonight she could not help herself.

Just as tears started to fill her eyes she was abruptly brought out of her reminiscing mood by the sound of Cleo barking at the door.

At first, she thought that it was the sound of the wind that had disturbed her dog, but the barking continued. Eventually, she was forced to get out of her chair to go and check. She decided to open the door, despite the blizzard that could be heard howling outside.

Cautiously, she opened the door just enough to peer into the thick gloom of the evening, stepping back in disbelief at what she saw.

It was a young boy standing on the porch. He appeared to be about six years old, and he was smiling at her. Then, in a quiet childlike voice, he said, "May I come in please?"

It took only seconds for her to get over the shock of seeing someone, let alone a small child, being out in this kind of weather, at this time of night.

Quickly opening the door a little more she ushered her visitor inside. Casting a glance at the path leading to her door, for a moment she was perplexed at the lack of footprints leading to her house. But, shaking her head, she assumed the wind had just blown away any trace of his tracks.

There appeared to be very little snow on her visitor's

clothes despite him having been out in the blizzard. Nor did he seem to be suffering from exposure to the cold at all.

"I will make you something warm to drink, what would you like?" Ann waited only a moment before continuing, "Then we can sit down and talk," she said.

"Thank you, hot chocolate would be very nice," her guest replied. "I will sit here on the floor by your dog while you prepare my drink, that is if you don't mind."

While warming the milk for his drink, Ann asked, "What is your name? We can talk later about how you came to be out in this weather, but I need to know what to call you."

"I am known as Leon," he replied, stroking the long floppy ears of the dog who was loving the unexpected attention.

A few minutes later, the chocolate was ready. Ann placed the mug carefully on the rug next to Leon then she sat back in her chair, looking intently at her caller.

She had a feeling of having met him before or of knowing him from somewhere. But, for some strange reason, she did not ask him this.

Still, she had so many other questions to ask. Why was he out on his own in this terrible weather, especially on Christmas Eve? Where did he come from?

However, suddenly, all the questions she intended to ask no longer seemed important. She just felt peculiarly satisfied in knowing his name.

Leon sat on the rug quietly, seemingly contented to be next to Cleo, who had curled up alongside him.

For some unknown reason, Ann found herself spending the evening talking to Leon about her past. She was comfortable talking to this child as if he was an adult, one she had known for a very long time.

"It is quite remarkable that you are here tonight, as I often have dreams of a little boy of a similar age to you. I know I tend to ramble on a bit but that's what happens when you live on your own and then you suddenly have someone to talk to."

She paused to see if Leon was interested and he appeared to be so as he smiled at her.

"I haven't always lived here on my own. I was once married and raised two wonderful sons. They grew into men that any mother would be proud of. Tragically the older one passed away several years ago."

Ann stopped as the sad memory of the loss of her son caused a small pain in her chest.

Then taking control she went on. "One of my fondest memories of them was actually when my youngest son was born. His brother, who was about your age, held him tightly in his arms, kissing him on the forehead, and saying that he would always love him, protect him, and watch over him." She smiled at the memory.

"He said that it was his job to forever look after his little brother, and I truly believe that he still does. It was such a special time. It was the happiest I had ever seen him in his young life."

Ann sighed, and then she said, "I often wonder what he looks like, now that he is in heaven. Is he still as handsome as what I remember, or has he aged like we do?

Leon stopped petting Cleo and looked up at Ann.

"I can only tell you what I believe," he said. "And that is, when your spirit goes to heaven you can choose whatever age you want to be, and most of them choose the age when they were the happiest. Listening to what you just told me tonight, then I am sure he would choose to be about six years old again."

Ann smiled, saying, "That is such a beautiful belief, Leon; you have such an old soul for someone so young."

Leon smiled warmly at her.

All the while she talked, Ann found she no longer needed to ask Leon anything about himself. It was as if there was no reason to do so. Instead, she just talked and talked, mostly about her sons.

During the evening, as she looked at Leon, she noticed the young boy was wearing a small ceramic badge on the lapel of his coat. It was of a red Welsh dragon, yet she did not feel a need to comment on it.

The evening quickly passed with Ann continuing to reminisce about her sons and about how proud she was of their achievements. Also, why she had chosen this life of solitude on this somewhat bleak mountain.

Eventually late into the evening, feeling relaxed and happy, she succumbed to tiredness and fell asleep, sitting upright in her chair.

* * * * *

Many hours later, she awoke shivering with cold. The fire had long ago gone out, and there were just a few glowing embers to remind her of yesterday evening.

Slowly, she focused her bleary eyes, expecting to see Leon sleeping next to Cleo, but there was only the still full mug of chocolate on the floor next to the dog. Leon was nowhere to be seen.

"It is Christmas morning," Ann said to the dog who was curled up next to her chair. "I know I have often said that nobody should be on their own on Christmas Eve. Was I longing for some company so much last night that I dreamt we had a visitor?"

With a puzzled frown, she looked at Cleo again.

"Mmm… but then why would I make a second drink? Our visitor seemed so real, yet it seems it has just been the two of us, hasn't it, Cleo?"

Buy now the snow had stopped falling, and if only to satisfy herself that last night hadn't happened, Ann opened the door to see if there were any footprints in the crisp snow on the path leading to her door.

There weren't any!

She smiled to herself.

"Maybe I have been living on my own for far too long, so now I am starting to imagine people," she said aloud.

Then laughing lightly, and looking at Cleo, she said, "At least I don't expect you to answer me! If you did then I would have to start worrying about my sanity," and she laughed again.

That afternoon, Ann prepared and ate a simple but traditional dinner, not forgetting to give an ample helping of turkey to Cleo.

Later, she once again sat down in her old armchair with

a nice hot cup of coffee. But, she could not help thinking about last night and slowly she began to convince herself that it had only been a dream.

"I suppose I am a silly old woman, aren't I?" she said addressing the dog resting near the hearth.

Cleo, however, merely opened her eyes slowly, then rolled over before standing up to wander over to her water bowl.

* * * * *

The snow finally stopped and the afternoon sun was starting to sink into the west. A final single shaft of light pierced the tiny window, coming to rest on a small object where Cleo had earlier been sleeping.

The object was a small badge of a red dragon.

"Am I still dreaming?" she said aloud, bending down to pick up the tiny badge.

It was at that very moment that she realised that Leon was the word Noel spelled backwards. And that in every language she knew, the translation of Noel into English meant Christmas.

Smiling, she finally accepted that she did indeed have a guest last night, and she now also knew who it had been.

"It wasn't a lonely Christmas after all was it, Cleo?" Ann

said aloud sounding contented with her lot.

For Jamie,

Lots of love, Dad

ABOUT THE AUTHOR

Lawrence Dracut (the writer's pen name), is a Welshman born and bred. He has travelled across the world, owning a variety of businesses, before finally retiring some ten years ago after a career as a Clinical Hypnotherapist and Counsellor. Since then, he has been able to pursue his passion for writing.

Although he loves writing children's books, published under the pen name of Sebastian Stumblebum, he can be somewhat cynical of society's failure to care for our planet. As such he deemed that his adult fiction, and environmental stories which sometimes have a sarcastic edge to them, are better published under his alter ego of Lawrence Dracut.

Poetry is also another side to his multifaceted personality.

www.lawrence-dracut.com   **www.sebastianstumblebum.com**

THE PUBLISHER

This book is published by Pen & Ink Designs Publishing, a small independent Welsh Publishing House based in Cardiff.

www.penandinkdesigns.co.uk